SHEPHERDS
of the
LOST

Family Secrets

SHEPHERDS
of the
LOST
Family Secrets

BY
JOSEPH & LEIGH RENZI

ISBN (Paperback): 979-8-9991356-0-5
Cover Illustration and Design by David Sean SanAngelo
Interior Book Design by Marta Dec

Published by Joseph & Leigh Renzi
Washington, D.C.
www.JosephLeighRenzi.com

Library of Congress Control Number: 2025914815
First Edition
Printed in the United States of America
10 9 8 7 6 5 4 3 2 1

For information about bulk purchases, school visits, or author
events, please contact: www.JosephLeighRenzi.com

For our children, who continuously remind us how wondrous life can be.

CONTENTS

PROLOGUE:

THE IN BETWEEN

The wind howled as Felix sat rigidly atop a massive hill, looking over the vast nothingness that lay before him. His white hair was matted from the cold rain and icicles formed around the edges of his face. Eons of ice had accumulated around the seat Felix rested on, degrading the wooden chair into a spiky, menacing mess. Like a king atop his throne, Felix inspected his domain with a shrewd eye. The land was dreary and barren, a mass of grays and beiges. The air was cold, and the ground was covered in a blanket of ice with patches of dirty, sludgy snow. Barely any light filtered through the fog that hung heavy in the air. The clouds overhead seemed to cry out as an ever-constant drizzle churned in every direction. Strangely, no matter the day and no matter the weather, the moment the rain made contact with the ground it nearly always froze.

Behind Felix sprawled a massive, dark castle. It was cold and intimidating, with dozens of spires each reaching their peak far out of sight, up and beyond the ominous clouds. Two massive doors, etched with what appeared to be creatures crying out in agony, stood tall and mighty in the center of the building. For all its might and intimidation, decay and rot ran rife beneath the grand façade.

Felix coughed a cold, wet cough, losing control for several seconds before clearing his throat. "You'd think I'd be used to this terrible weather by now." He tapped his fingers in annoyance against the icy chair's arm. "This place is miserably cold. Even for me." He turned his head toward the castle. "And these house guests have no manners. Still raising such a ruckus, even after all these years. Will they never learn?"

"Hmph," a deep voice replied in his ear. "It is time, my Keeper, time for us to finally return to your home."

"What are you talking about, Pride?" an irritated Felix snarled. "We go there all the time and take whatever we want."

"No, no, Felix. This is not what I mean," Pride's hollow, otherworldly voice responded. "It is time for us to return to where we first met. To where your journey first began. To your hometown of Foggy Hollows."

"Return to Foggy Hollows, you say?" Felix strummed his fingers deliberately one by one against the ice. As each finger hit the frozen chair, the arm of it cracked more and more beneath the force of his strength.

"You've waited long enough, Felix. We need to finish what we started and rid ourselves of the remaining Shepherds." Pride paused to let his words sink in and then continued. "Don't tell me you're still scared of your sister and what she did to you last time."

Felix sprang to his feet and picked up the chair, ripping it from the ground where it had been frozen in place for an eternity. The cracking ice sounded as if it was shrieking in pain as he broke the throne free. Felix lifted the massive chair high into the air and slammed it onto the ground. It splintered into thousands of small pieces.

"Did I hit a nerve?" Pride laughed mockingly.

The air grew even more frigid as the rain turned into snow. Felix closed his eyes and began slowly waving his arms back and forth through the air. The vast layers of ice that covered the ground began to expand and crack, creating a hollow, echoing sound. The singing ice reverberated and boomed throughout the kingdom, becoming louder and louder with each note. The noises were so inexplicably strange and otherworldly, it was as if ancient beings were awakening from a slumber beneath the ice's surface. Like a conductor guiding the sweet symphony of his orchestra, Felix moved his hands and swayed back and forth in harmony with the hauntingly beautiful melody. When Felix finished his performance, he took a solemn bow.

"Foggy Hollows," he repeated slowly, recalling a life from long ago. "Yes, I think you're right. It's time we return home."

"Your sister will be waiting for you," Pride said condescendingly, looking Felix over with challenging eyes.

"Esmeralda. Yes, I'm sure she will be. In fact, I'm counting on it." His eyes went entirely black as a smirk crept across one side of his mouth. "Let the war begin."

CHAPTER 1:

THE SNAKE BITE

"Nobody invited you, Zach. Go away!" Vidia said, her cheeks flushed with embarrassment as she shoved the boy from behind the rope swing.

"Vidia, he was just kidding. Why not let him stay?" Aurelia interjected, watching from above as she sat on a tree branch.

Vidia just shook her head in response. She didn't know Zach very well, but she knew she'd had enough of him. Her best friend Aurelia thought he was nice enough, but that was the only reason Vidia tolerated his company. This evening, he'd waltzed into Vidia's yard while she was relaxing on her rope swing and had the nerve to ask her if she thought she was too old for a swing. After she'd hopped off her swing in embarrassment,

Zach immediately grabbed the swaying swing and plopped himself right on it. "Trick question! You're never too old for a swing," he'd said with a laugh, enjoying himself at Vidia's expense. *He always does stuff like this*, Vidia thought, and continued pushing at him.

"It's ok, Aurelia, Vidia just likes pushing me on the swing," Zach teased. "It's really nice of you, but I'm big enough to do it myself."

Aurelia couldn't help but laugh at the scene. Zach was easily a full head taller than Vidia, and there was no way she would be able to push him off the swing.

"I'm not giving you a push, I'm shoving you off!" Vidia objected.

"That's fine, I don't think there's really any difference," Zach replied as he swung back and forth.

"I'm not kidding around. GET. OFF. NOW!" Vidia yelled, causing Aurelia to startle and nearly fall from the tree. As she stumbled and caught her balance, her large glasses fell off her face and onto the ground below.

Surprised at Vidia's response, Zach jumped off the swing and went sailing into the air. He landed on his feet with a thump and turned around to give a quick wave. "I didn't know it was that serious. I was just messing around. See you guys later," he said as he climbed onto his bike and rode off.

"Sorry! And see you tomorrow," Aurelia yelled after him.

"Good riddance," Vidia snapped, making sure she was loud enough for Zach to hear. She turned to her friend and crossed her arms. "Why do you keep inviting him over?" Vidia asked angrily.

"I saw him outside on my way over, and he asked to join us. He's always been nice to us. I don't understand why you get so upset with him," Aurelia said, puzzled. She climbed down from the tree, picked up her glasses and shrugged as she put them back on. "Anyway, what do you want to do now?"

"Nothing. I'm sure my mom will call me in for dinner any minute," Vidia said irritably.

"Oh, ok. Well, I guess I'll head home too," Aurelia said. She knew that when Vidia got in one of her moods, she'd better let her friend cool off.

"See you tomorrow then?" Vidia questioned as Aurelia climbed on her bike.

"Tomorrow is good. Toodles!" Aurelia said cheerfully as she rode away.

Vidia sat down on the swing, relieved to finally be alone. She wasn't very social even though she wished she could be. She noticed the seat was still warm from Zach sitting there moments earlier. "Gross," she muttered, annoyed as she began swaying back and forth. The rope swing hung from an enormous live oak tree. Dad installed it the summer before last, hoping it would entice Vidia to spend more time outside. His plan worked, as the wooden swing he'd built with Vidia was now her favorite place to spend her time and held a special place in her heart.

The tree's massive branches shot out from the trunk in all directions, twisting and turning. Some of the branches dipped all the way to the ground before climbing back up into the sky. Vidia's front yard was quite large, but the grand old tree stood out as the centerpiece, towering high above the house. It's extensive canopy of branches offered shade that covered a substantial part of the ground. The massive trunk splintered into multiple limbs near the base, which made climbing it quite easy. It was late October, and Spanish moss dripped from the large limbs, creating a sorrowful, haunting look in the cool evening air.

Vidia held the ropes of the swing loosely in her hands as she swung back and forth, her feet scuffing the ground below as she floated in the dying day-light. Now that Aurelia and Zach were gone, Vidia quickly became lost in thought, thinking about her growing family. Vidia wasn't sure if she wanted to be a big sister. She'd enjoyed the perks of being an only child for the past eleven years. Sure, there were times when she had thought it would be fun to have a little brother or sister to play with, but now that the family's newest addition was set to arrive any day, Vidia thought she'd be happier waiting another eleven years. Or better yet, no sibling at all, thanks.

Why didn't Mom and Dad ask me if I wanted a sibling before they went and had another? Why wasn't

I included in this decision? she wondered, drifting back and forth on the swing in the shade of the tree.

Halloween was only one week away, and she worried this baby was going to make his or her grand entrance just in time to keep Vidia's pillow-case void of candy and her creepy witch costume hanging in the closet. Mom was already two days past due. *There's nothing fashionable about being late,* Vidia thought to herself. *What a rude and selfish little potato.* She laughed at the visual she had created in her mind, but the more she stewed in her troubled thoughts, the angrier she became with her parents.

Had she told them about her concerns, had she made them aware of her reservations? No, of course not. When they told her they had a sur-prise, she was excited. She thought it was the trip to Disney World they'd been talking about for years. Then when they told her the "good" news, all she felt was a sense of dread. She wanted to let all her fears come tumbling out, but she couldn't bear to wipe the joyful looks off her parents' faces. Plus, if she shared her feelings, she figured it would have caused another silly "teaching moment" as her mom liked to say. And Dad, he'd ramble on about how important family is and how this would be an opportunity for her to learn to share. *No. I'm not interested in hearing any of that,* she thought. So instead, Vidia had blankly stared back at her mother when the news was shared and said the first thing that popped into her head: "Isn't that just yummy." *That was kind of weird, why did I say that?* she thought, but then imagined the chubby cheeks of a newborn and giggled to herself, throwing her head back in the breeze.

Although Vidia did not know it, the news of a baby had been a surprise to her parents, Frank and Charlotte, as well. Her father's eyes filled with tears of joy when Charlotte had shared the news with him. Frank always wanted more children, so he was elated and could not wait for the baby's arrival. Charlotte had cried too, but her tears were that of fear and not joy. She felt she could hardly shield Vidia from the dangers of the world and was certain she couldn't ever bear double the worry, double the responsibility, of protecting another child. She decided many years ago, somewhat disappointedly, that it was best for her not to have any more children. Charlotte once dreamed of having a big family, but that changed when she lost her lifelong best friend, Annabelle, and Annabelle's husband, Victor, to a monstrous darkness that festers in the shadows of our world. She had nearly lost Vidia too, who was only three years old at the time.

Charlotte's fears were partially subdued when she saw the excitement in Frank's face at the news. She knew, despite her reservations, this baby had the most devoted father she could have ever imagined. As the months of her pregnancy wore on, Charlotte slowly began to warm to the idea of having another child. Now that the baby could come any day, her excitement was palpable. She would protect this baby, just as she protected Vidia, and everything would be fine.

Vidia, on the other hand, still couldn't shake the feeling that somehow this baby was going to replace her, even though she knew it was probably a silly thought. Vidia did not like surprises, and the news of this baby was a huge surprise. Worst of all, her parents decided to keep the surprises coming. They weren't even going to find out if it was a boy or a girl until the slimy little bundle of joy made its glorious arrival. Vidia's cheeks deepened to a shade of crimson as she continued to stew. "Let's be honest, does anybody actually want a sibling?" she mumbled to herself, but she knew the answer was yes, and she wondered why she felt so differently.

Her mind continued to wander through the possibilities. *A boy. That could be fine,* she tried to convince herself. *Sure, he'd likely be dirty, grimy, smelly, and cry all the time, but he'd be cute, wouldn't he?*

A girl, though, Vidia pondered. *That would definitely be worse. There is nothing joyful about having to share all my stuff with a snot-nosed slimy slug.* She shook her head, wondering why she had such negative feelings towards this baby, but she continued to spiral. *A baby girl could replace me, and at the very least take all my parents' attention away from me,* she concluded. *I won't stand for that, no, not at all. I could maybe learn to live with a grimy, smelly little brother. But if Mom and Dad bring home a girl, I don't know what I'll do.*

Unbeknownst to Vidia, a massive vulture sat perched in wait atop the highest branch of the live oak tree. Its red, otherworldly eyes glared directly down at Vidia. The creature's beak remained oddly agape as it watched her intently. The more Vidia stewed, the bigger the bird's eyes grew, and the wider it opened its mouth. It almost looked as if it enjoyed the turmoil festering within Vidia.

Feelings of envy pulsed through Vidia as she thought about a faceless little baby taking attention away from her. She clenched her hands tightly around the thick rope of the swing, unable to think about anything else.

Despite her troubled thoughts, Vidia looked like a typical eleven-year-old girl. She was of average height with a slender build. She wore her long, shiny, dark brown hair in a ponytail to keep it tamed and away from her face. Her thin lips were usually pursed tightly together, giving her a very severe expression, and her eyebrows were perpetually furrowed as if deep in an uncomfortable thought. Her bright green eyes slanted upwards at the corners, giving her a striking appearance that had a way of captivating her audience.

She stared at her house, wondering if there would be enough room for everyone and everything once the baby came. The spare bedroom she had taken over had already been redone and replaced with a nursery. Her belongings that used to sit in that room had been moved to the dark, gloomy basement. Dad assured her that their house had more than enough space for a family of four. He went so far as to say it could even fit a couple more children if ever needed. Dad's words, while well-intended, lately had the opposite effect on Vidia. This instance was one of the worst yet.

One sibling sounds hard enough. More than one sibling, that would be some kind of wicked torture, Vidia thought.

Vidia had been so lost in thought, she didn't notice the comfortable cool daytime air had been replaced with the chill of twilight. The chill was nothing new to Vidia. The town of Foggy Hollows was known for being colder than all the surrounding towns, something no one seemed to be able to explain. This evening, though, had a particularly chilly bite. The setting sun cast a reddish glow about her house and yard, and a breeze picked up the heady scent of autumn. Vidia breathed in deeply. What was it she was smelling? *That's the smell of rot,* she thought, craning her head to the side, eyeing the pile of leaves her dad had raked earlier. She took another deep breath, enjoying the scent of the decay.

As she dragged her feet on the ground, she noticed something moving in the grass below her. She brought the swing to a stop and leaned forward, trying to get a better look at what was slinking toward her.

Is it a broken tree limb? Why would a branch look like it was moving? My eyes must be playing tricks on me in the setting sun, she thought.

All at once, the object she thought to be a stick twisted and sprang up at her, and Vidia felt a sharp pain course through her ankle, leg, and then entire body. Realizing it was an enormous snake, she screamed and jumped off the swing, her eyes squarely fixed on the large serpent. The snake was a muddy brown and looked like it was smiling as its tongue flickered in and out of its contorted mouth. When the serpent sprang again, this time Vidia was ready. She swiftly moved to the left, dodging the snake's attack, and ran inside yelling for her mom and dad.

"What happened?" her mom asked, looking down at the two puncture wounds on her daughter's ankle in the brightly lit living room.

"A snake bit me!" Vidia answered through tears. "It was watching me and pounced like a lion. It was so creepy. It went in to bite again, but I got away just in time."

"Where were you when it bit you?" Dad asked, entering the room with a look of worry.

"On the swing," said Vidia.

"I'm going to try and find it," Dad said, rushing out of the room.

"Does it hurt?" Mom asked, grabbing the first aid kit off the shelf and instructing Vidia to sit on the couch. Once they were both seated, Mom began dabbing it gently with a wet soapy cotton round. Despite Mom's cool and calm exterior, Vidia noticed a tremor in her mother's hands.

"It burns," Vidia replied, looking up at her mother.

The resemblance between Vidia and Charlotte was unmistakable. They both had the exact same tilted, striking green eyes, high cheekbones, and smooth dark brown hair that glistened with hints of red in the sunlight. Nearly every physical attribute Vidia bore either came from her mother, or her mother's side of the family, the Hartmans.

Charlotte had a true kindness about her face, but almost wore a weary look, as if she had lived much longer than her thirty-five years of age. Sometimes Vidia noticed a melancholy expression in her mother's eyes as her father spoke of their past years as a young married couple, and she wondered what her mother was thinking about. As a child, Charlotte had struggled with the same shortcomings that Vidia now dealt with, although anyone who knew Charlotte now would find it impossible to believe she was once reckless, quick-tempered, and very envious. Charlotte's whole world changed after her best friend's untimely death. Riddled with guilt and shame, Charlotte fell into a state of despair. Eventually she climbed her way out of this dark hole, but after the loss of her friend, she became an extremely reserved, private woman. Still, the one thing she was not able to mask was her constant worry that something terrible could happen at any moment.

Vidia's father, on the other hand, was an easy-going man and had always been so. He had dirty blond hair, hazel eyes, and a strong, square jawline. He was traditionally handsome in every sense of the word. Dad's was a calm, cool personality, slow to anger, and always seemed to be in a good mood as far as Vidia could tell.

The old saying of opposites attract was very much true in this instance. Her parents' bond was so strong that Vidia had never seen them so much as argue. They brought out the best in each other and believed, more than anything, that family came first. Frank saw so much of Charlotte in Vidia, and he was immensely proud of his smart, beautiful, and determined daughter. Vidia had a deep love of tradition, and a stalwart loyalty to the small circle of people she trusted. Frank could sense a great deal of anxiety in his daughter hiding beneath her angry outbursts. These outbursts had grown significantly since they had shared the news with Vidia of her mother's pregnancy. This worried both Frank and Charlotte, but Frank was confident that Vidia would warm to her little brother or sister once he or she arrived.

"Why is Dad trying to find the snake? He might end up getting bit, too," Vidia asked.

"He needs to find it to make sure it's not venomous. If he can't find it, or if he does and it is venomous, we'll need to take you to the hospital." Something flashed in Charlotte's eyes, and her anxiety grew. "It's ok, it will all be ok," she said, taking a deep breath as she attempted to calm herself. Slowly, the tremor in her hand ceased. "What color was the snake? Did it have any odd markings on its head?" she questioned urgently.

"It was brown," Vidia responded.

"Did it have a red spot on its forehead?" Mom asked again with worry in her voice.

"I don't know, I didn't see one," Vidia said, confused.

"There's a brown snake crawling on the driveway," Dad said, reentering the room. "Looks like a typical garden snake to me, except that it's big, real big. Probably more than six feet long. Never seen—"

Mom interrupted, looking at Dad with panic in her eyes. "Frank, does it have a red marking on its forehead?"

"I didn't notice one. What type of snake would that be?" Dad replied with a puzzled look.

"We need to be sure. Go check again," Mom demanded.

A bit confused, but seeing the worry in Mom's eyes, Dad responded, "Ok, sure, I'll double check."

Dad went back outside and returned a couple minutes later. "The snake's not in the driveway anymore. I looked all over the yard and can't find it anywhere. He's gone, but don't worry, Charlotte, it was a harmless brown garden snake. Nothing new, we get them all the time. A big one for sure, and the rodents better watch out, but we're fine. Promise," Dad said with confidence.

"You didn't sound so sure earlier," Mom said as she twisted her hands nervously.

"I'm sure it's fine. And we'll keep an eye on the snake bite," Dad said, trying to calm Charlotte.

Mom sighed as she rubbed Vidia's back. "So, there was no red marking on its forehead?" she asked once more.

"I would have noticed that. Everything will be fine. We just need to keep the wound clean," Dad responded in a soothing voice.

Vidia felt a touch of disappointment at the news, as she so craved the spotlight, and a venomous bite would have made her the center of attention for days, much more so than a non-venomous bite. Seeing the sad look on his daughter's face, Frank continued, "What do you say after dinner we pick a new book to start reading together? It's been a few weeks since we finished reading the last one."

"That's a great idea," Vidia agreed, forgetting about the snake bite.

After dinner, they all made their way to the living room. Vidia walked over to the old built-in shelves that lined the far end of the living room with a particular book in mind. Her parents had an enormous collection of books, many antique and handed down to them from relatives. Vidia spent many bored hours over the years eyeing the collection and skimming novels. It didn't take any time for her to spot what she was looking for.

"I've wanted to read this one for a while now," she

said, pulling a worn leather copy of Mary Shelley's *Frankenstein* off the shelf.

"Ah, yes. Very good choice, and what better time with Halloween just around the corner to read *Frankenstein*," Dad said, raising his arms and taking long lurching steps toward Vidia.

Mom and Vidia laughed in unison at Dad's imitation of Frankenstein's monster. "I haven't read that one since I was about your age, Vidia. Let's do it," Mom agreed.

Vidia raced back to the couch and plunked herself down on it and crossed her legs. "Dad, you read the first chapter and Mom can read the second. Then I'll read the third, fourth, and maybe fifth depending on how long we want to read for."

Dad and Mom both laughed. Dad turned off all the bright lights nearby, leaving only a small lamp on to create an appropriate ambiance for a scary story. He sat down and snuggled up to Mom as Vidia handed him the book. Frank cleared his throat, opened it to page one and began reading. Dad's voice always became dignified and theatrical when he began reading out loud. Everyone always remarked that he could have been a sportscaster or radio personality with his booming, polished tone.

Vidia took a throw blanket off the arm of the couch, wrapped it around herself and leaned back, propping her legs up over her mom's lap. The slow, sweet pitter-patter of a light rain began, enveloping Vidia as if in a hug and warming her to the core. Finally calm, the thought of the baby popped back into her head. Vidia imagined that the following week they'd again be cuddled up on the couch together reading, but rather than a family of three, they'd be a family of four. She smiled at the thought of a baby sitting on her lap, and for a moment she felt at peace. As she relaxed, an unexpected sharp pulse of pain coursed through her ankle where she had been bitten. With this, the momentary peace she felt vanished and a loathing crept into the corners of her mind. Vidia tried to push away the bad feelings, but she couldn't and worried these evenings might very well be coming to an end once the new baby came.

CHAPTER 2:

Echoes in the Attic

Vidia climbed the rickety stairs of the drop-down ladder and stepped into the attic, walking as lightly as possible to make sure nobody could hear her from below. *This is exciting*, she thought to herself. She loved rummaging through the collections of dusty boxes from years past, but didn't get the opportunity very often. The thrill of doing something that was against the rules added to the allure. The attic was easily her favorite part of the house.

This time, Vidia was on a specific mission. She didn't like the sparkly witch's hat that came with her Halloween costume and wanted something different. She knew that Mom had dressed up as a witch for Halloween multiple times as a child and was hoping there might be a witch's hat stashed somewhere in the piles of attic clutter. She remembered playing with old costumes with Mom years ago, but couldn't remember what part of the attic she kept them in. She shined a flashlight from one end of the room to the other, looking for the oldest boxes. *Ah ha! There they are.* She stepped over the Christmas decorations and walked to the very back of the attic. There were at least a dozen boxes all marked CHARLOTTE—CHILDHOOD.

How does she have so much stuff up here? Vidia felt a surge of anger. *And Mom says I have too many things? I can't believe she forces me to donate toys to children in need every Thanksgiving to teach me compassion. Next Thanksgiving I'll donate all this stuff and see how she likes it.* As Vidia began sifting through the boxes, the fear of getting caught crept into her mind. *I'll never be able to go through it all before Mom or Dad notices what I'm doing.* She briefly debated going downstairs and asking Mom for help but decided against it. She knew that she'd get in trouble for going into the attic and digging through everything without permission. Mom always acted so strange and nervous about Vidia going into the attic. *Like I'm some sort of baby that can't take care of myself. The irony is I can get into the attic way easier than Mom right now. She's so pregnant she can barely climb our stairs without stopping for a break. If I asked her to look for the hat she'd take forever. It would probably be Halloween before she even had the energy to look. Nope. I'll find it myself. Better to ask for forgiveness than permission.* She smiled and nodded, sure of her decision.

She rummaged through the boxes as quickly as possible. As she pushed box after box to the side, a large wooden chest came into view. *I've never noticed this before. Has Mom been hiding it?* She opened the chest, her eyes wide with anticipation and her mind racing with possibilities. Much to her disappointment, the chest was completely empty. *Are you kidding me? What a letdown,* Vidia thought irritably, and she slammed the chest closed in indignation, too upset to care how loud she was. *Why would such a big chest be up here in this cluttered attic with nothing in it?*

As the chest thumped shut, she heard another thud from within the chest that seemed to echo over and over. A strange sensation overtook her, and she felt as if the reverberation was calling to her, demanding her attention. Vidia reopened the chest, puzzled, and much to her surprise, it now held a black box within it. *How is this possible?* As if on cue, she heard an ominous creaking sound from the underside of the chest's lid and turned her neck to look up at it. *There's a trap door,* she thought as she opened and shut the secret compartment, causing it to creak again. *Woah. This chest must be for hiding things!* Vidia was thrilled. She'd never seen anything like this.

Her attention quickly shifted back to the smaller box that had fallen from within the trap door. *This is gonna be good*, she thought as she shined the flashlight on it. Vidia inspected the rectangular black wooden box and noticed it appeared to be quite dated. *Was this even Mom's?* The words SHADOWS OF THE PAST were deeply engraved into the top of the box. Vidia ran her fingers over top the rough texture of the writing and pondered. The antiquated, mystical appearance pleased her. It looked like the box folded open from the middle, but as she tried to pull it apart, it barely budged. When she looked closer, she noticed the two initials FS neatly carved into the center of the box. *Who could that be?* Squinting in the dim light, she saw a tiny keyhole below the initials that was barely visible.

She turned back to the chest and stuck her hand deep within the secret compartment, hoping to find a key. She felt a pocket within the chamber and pushed her arm deeper inside. "Ow!" she yelled, pulling her hand out as she gasped and covered her mouth, afraid she had been heard. Something sharp had pricked her finger deep within the depths of the chest. A small but steady stream of blood trickled from her finger onto her jeans and the floor below. She was so intrigued by her discovery she barely noticed her cut, and reached back into the pocket with her other hand, running her finger more gingerly across the sharp object this time until she felt a blunt end. She grabbed at it greedily and pulled it out. Much to her delight, it was a large knife. One end was sharp and had a couple teeth of differing lengths just below the point. The other end was clearly a handle with a leather strap. *Could this be the key?* she wondered. She inserted it into the keyhole and turned. It clicked as it unlocked without any resistance, and Vidia grinned from ear to ear, pleased with her discovery.

She opened the box to find a shiny black and gray moon in the middle of the board. Vidia ran her hands across it and realized that it was made of marbled stone. Her hand lingered on the board and an odd coldness swept over her. There were two black candleholders on the top corners of the board, and below each one was a long, skinny red candle bound to the box with a leather strap. Both candles had clearly been used but had plenty of life left in them.

Vidia picked up the candle on the left side of the box and noticed an inscription written into the wood beneath it. She squinted, struggling with the tiny print under her flashlight. BURN BOTH CANDLES TO REACH THE LOST. ASK YOUR QUESTIONS TWICE OVER. LET THE FLAMES AND THE SHADOWS LIGHT YOUR PATH. YOU NEVER KNOW WHAT MAY ANSWER FROM THE IN BETWEEN. Vidia read the instructions over twice. "In between?" she asked herself, confused. Then she turned her attention to the lower right-hand corner of the Shadow Box where a small drawer resided. She opened it, revealing a used box of matches, and a folded-up piece of worn paper. She gently unfolded the paper, and much to her excitement, found a handwritten note. She read the faded words to herself with bated breath.

Do not cower from the shadows, instead embrace and use them to your advantage. There is great power to be found in all that is feared. Keep this Shadow Box our little secret.

Your friend, F

Vidia folded the paper back up, unsure what to make of it, and put it back in the drawer. She laid the palm of her hand back on the marble stone, relishing the strange, icy sensation, deep in thought. *I wonder where this came from. Just wait until I show this to Aurelia! She is going to be so creeped out,* Vidia thought to herself excitedly. The flashlight flickered for a moment, and Vidia felt her blood run cold, a sudden eerie chill in her bones.

"Vidia! Dinner time," Mom called from downstairs, her voice reverberating through the attic and startling Vidia. She closed the Shadow Box in a panic as quickly as she could, her fingers shaking. She tucked it under her arm and frantically put everything else back in its proper place. After sloppily finishing, she turned toward the exit and the light from her flashlight danced on something metal shimmering at the top of an old laundry basket. Distracted but still in a rush, Vidia ran up to the dancing reflection, reached into the mound of clothing and grabbed at it. *Here it is! Mom's witch's hat!* She shined her flashlight on it. The black hat had a large purple buckle that sat just above the wide brim and glittered under the flashlight's beam.

This is perfect! The purple buckle even matches my costume! she thought.

"Vidia, where are you? Dinner time!" Vidia put the hat on her head, bolted across the attic with the Shadow Box still in tow, raced down the ladder, and ran into her room. She shoved the Shadow Box under her bed and out of sight.

"Vidia, why is the attic open?" Mom demanded, now standing at the top of the hallway staircase and very much out of breath.

"Sorry, Mom. I needed a hat to go with my costume, and I know you have all those old outfits up there. I didn't want to make you climb any more stairs than you have to right now. You know, being pregnant and everything." Vidia forced a smile and hoped her mom would buy her explanation. "I was trying to help you out," she added, trying her hardest to sound sweet.

Mom wasn't so easily fooled. "You know you're not allowed to go into the attic on your own! What has gotten into you lately?" She paused and then continued with an air of trepidation. "Did you see anything?"

"What do you mean? Look at me!" she posed with her hat and grinned.

Mom laughed. "Yes, I can see that."

"Isn't it cool?" Vidia pulled the hat off and admired it. Mom took the hat from Vidia's outstretched hands and looked at it longingly. "I remember this one. It really is one of a kind."

"Can I please have it? Pretty please? I love it," Vidia pleaded.

"Yes, that's fine. Did you find anything else up there?"

"Lots of other clothes, but this was all I took," Vidia said, placing the hat back on her head.

"Alright. Come on down for dinner. The food is getting cold. And after that, you're going straight to bed."

"But why?" Vidia protested, bending down and scratching at her ankle.

"You went into the attic without permission when we've been over this before. Your actions have consequences, Vidia. And for heaven's sake, don't scratch at your snake bite. It will get infected."

"It's fine. I'll scratch it if I want to," Vidia responded coldly and began to stomp off.

Worry began to take hold in Charlotte's mind. "Let me take a look at it."

"I already said it's fine," Vidia snapped.

"Right now, or you're about to get in even bigger trouble," Mom warned.

Vidia pulled her sock down, revealing the two small puncture wounds. Much to Charlotte's relief, the two small slits had already scabbed over and the cut looked to be healing properly. "Good, very good.

No cause for concern. Just don't scratch." Charlotte sighed with relief.

"See, I told you," Vidia retorted. "Why do you worry so much?"

Ignoring her daughter's rude words, Charlotte simply pointed down the stairs towards the kitchen. "Go eat. Then straight to bed."

"V? Wake up, honey!" Although Vidia was wide awake, she didn't budge, still angry that she was sent to bed early.

"Mom and I need to go to the hospital. You're going to be a big sister," Dad continued, gently shaking his daughter's arm.

"Grandma should be here any minute. She'll hang out with you for the next couple days until we come home. Isn't this exciting? Come say bye to Mom."

Vidia *hated* being called V. She'd told her dad that a million times. *Why doesn't he ever listen?* she wondered to herself, still pretending to be asleep.

Shortcuts—that's what nicknames represent. Dad is so focused on this stupid baby that he's calling me V to save a split second. And now he wants me to come say goodbye? Not interested, she thought, silently seething.

"Frank? Frank? Your mother is here," Charlotte called.

Dad kissed Vidia on the forehead. "All right, honey, you can keep resting. We'll be back in a couple days. I love you so much. Have fun with Grandma," Dad said, and left Vidia's bedroom.

Vidia got up and crept quietly over to her bedroom door, eavesdropping on her parents and Grandma as they whispered at the bottom of the staircase. As she listened, the snake bite on her ankle started itching intensely. She tried her hardest not to scratch it but couldn't help herself. She made a point to only scratch around the bite, so as not to disturb the scabs, but this did not relieve her itch. She scratched more and more furiously until she was worried her parents might hear the noise from downstairs. Vidia was too distracted with her parents and grandmother's conversation to notice the pus pockets that were beginning to form around the edges of the scabs on her ankle.

"She didn't want to get up?" Mom asked with disappointment in her voice.

"No," Dad replied, looking dejected. "She was pretending to be asleep, as if it's Sunday and she doesn't want to get up for church."

"I always thought she'd love having a sibling. I don't understand her attitude," Mom sighed.

"Oh, you two are overreacting. Of course, she'll love him or her. She just needs to meet the little bugger! Then you'll see, she'll be enamored with her new sibling. You'll end up wishing she'd just let the baby be sometimes!" Grandma said with a laugh.

"I hope you're right, Mom. I worry we've spoiled her too much," whispered Dad, unable to hide the look of concern on his face.

"Well, Frank, don't you worry. You can leave the spoiling to me. That's what grandmas are for. Now you two better get going."

Just then, Mom started breathing heavily, grabbed onto Frank's shoulder and groaned in pain.

"Charlotte, Mom's right. It's time to go," Dad said, rubbing her back.

Charlotte nodded her head in agreement. "Let me go say goodbye to Vidia, and then we can head out."

Mom started up the stairs, and Vidia ran back to her room and jumped into bed. Hoping her mom didn't hear the bed creaking, she climbed under the covers.

Mom sat down next to Vidia's bed and put her hand on her back.

"I know you're awake, honey. Can you give me a kiss goodbye? This is the last time I'll see you before you're a big sister."

Vidia paused. She did love her mom, and could tell this moment meant a lot to her. Vidia turned to face her, and her mother began to smile as their eyes met.

"V, you're going to be such a good big sister. I just know it," Mom said.

There it is again, Vidia thought to herself. *Another ridiculous shortcut by one of my lazy parents so they don't have to spend as much time with me.* The baby wasn't even here yet, but things were already different.

Vidia looked at her mom and narrowed her eyes. "My name is Vidia," she said, hands clenched together in an attempt to contain her anger. She turned her back to her mother and pulled the covers over her head.

Mom let out another low gasp of pain. Vidia wondered if this was the baby already stealing the show, or if maybe she finally had gotten her point across to her mom.

"Charlotte, we need to go," Dad called up the stairs.

Mom pulled the blanket down a couple inches, kissed the back of Vidia's head, and walked out of the room.

As Vidia heard the car start outside, she got up and started pacing the room, biting her fingernails. She knew it was a bad habit, but Mom wasn't there to tell her to stop. *Well, at least there's that,* Vidia thought as she peeked through the blinds to watch her parents fade into the distance. A part of her wanted to run outside and tell them to wait, to give her mom a big hug and say she was sorry. But her momentary remorse was gone as quickly as it had come. Vidia realized the next time she saw her parents, they'd have that horrid little troll with them.

"It better be a boy troll," Vidia said to herself. "And he better not ruin Halloween for me." Vidia slipped and bit a little too far down on her nail, sending a sharp shooting pain through her thumb. "Ow," she whispered. She squeezed her thumb as hard as she could with her other hand, creating a little pool of blood on the side of her nail. She eyed the blood, intrigued, and began sucking it off her thumb.

Vidia caught her reflection in the mirror, realizing she herself looked like a thumb sucking baby, and was suddenly glad she was alone. The odd, warm, metallic taste soothed her. She lay down to go back to sleep, sucking her bloody thumb until she drifted off into a troubled slumber.

CHAPTER 3:

THE WAITING GAME

In the morning, Vidia woke, hoping the night before had been a dream. She jumped out of bed and ran downstairs, expecting to find breakfast and her mom and dad waiting for her.

"Good morning, sleepyhead. I was beginning to think you didn't want to hang out with me," Grandma said with a smile.

"Hi, Grandma, nice to see you." Vidia's words were genuine. Her grandma always made her feel special. Vidia wished she could be more like her sometimes. Grandma could find the fun in anything with such a sunny disposition. In all of Vidia's eleven years, she couldn't think of a time she'd ever seen her grandma upset. Maybe today would be fun, after all.

"Does this mean Mom and Dad are at the hospital?"

"Yes, honey. You ready to be a big sister?" Grandma asked.

"No!" Surprised at her own honesty, Vidia continued, "Well, not sure."

"Hmm, I've been there, too. I remember back when my younger sister Margaret was born. I really didn't know what to think." She paused.

"Well, what happened?" Vidia asked impatiently.

"Of course we fought every now and then, but she became my best friend. We got into all kinds of trouble growing up together. She was my maid of honor when I married your granddad. We still talk on the phone most every day."

The only person Vidia considered a friend was Aurelia. They lived in the same neighborhood and went to Sunday school together. Vidia's parents were close to Aurelia's grandmother, Mrs. Santiago, and Mom had grown up with Aurelia's mother, Annabelle. Apparently the two of them were best friends their whole lives until both Annabelle and her husband Victor passed away. Aurelia and Vidia were only toddlers when all of this happened, much too young to remember any of it. Vidia didn't know what happened to Aurelia's parents, and whenever she asked about it, Mom would become teary eyed and tight lipped. The only thing that was clear to Vidia was that they must have died under strange circumstances. Oddly enough, Aurelia was also completely unaware of what had happened to her parents. Whenever she asked her abuela, little information was provided. Mrs. Santiago would say, "I'll tell you once you're older, mija, once you're ready."

"Ready for what? I don't understand," Aurelia would complain to Vidia. The secrecy both disturbed and confused the two girls. They conducted all sorts of research and snooped whenever and wherever they could. Still, there was no indication of what had happened. One thing was for certain, though, Mrs. Santiago was definitely hiding something, and Mom knew more than she let on.

Aurelia felt more like a cousin than just a friend, and the two families even spent most holidays together. Vidia understood her friendship with Aurelia probably wouldn't even exist had it not been for their parents, but better a forced friendship than no friends at all.

Realizing how lost in thought she'd become, Vidia finally responded to her grandma. "Another friend, that would be nice. I'd like that."

"I just don't understand why you keep to yourself so much, Vidia. Life's more fun with friends."

"I don't know, Grandma. I'm not like the other kids," Vidia said, pouring herself a bowl of cereal.

"Sure you are, honey, you just need to learn to be more considerate. You've been an only child for so many years. I know it's not easy for you to share."

There it was. The judgment Vidia had felt for the past nine months from her parents, and here it was again, but this time coming from Grandma. The scabbed wound on her ankle suddenly throbbed as Grandma's words pricked at her heart.

Vidia slammed her spoon into the cereal bowl, spilling milk onto the table.

"I can share just fine," she said through gritted teeth. "I just like attention. What's wrong with that?"

"Nothing, hon. You just need to learn to share that attention. You should *want* to share that attention," Grandma concluded. "Now quit the backtalk and clean up that mess you made. I'll be in the family room when you're done, if you want to come join me. We can play cards if you'd like."

Vidia bit her tongue, as playing cards with Grandma was one of her favorite things to do.

Grandma winked at Vidia as if to say *checkmate,* and left the room.

Vidia stared at her cereal, watching the once crunchy meal become soggy and gross. *More judgment,* she thought, *and worst of all it was coming from Grandma!* She swallowed her anger. *I can fix this. I just need to calm myself.* She scarfed the rest of her cereal down without chewing to avoid the soggy texture, cleaned up the milk spill, and hurried into the family room to make things right with Grandma.

Vidia found Grandma parked on the couch, twisting and turning two oversized needles again and again with yarn. "What are you doing?" she asked curiously.

"I'm making a baby blanket for your new sibling."

"I thought we were going to play cards," Vidia replied, trying to stay calm.

"Sorry, honey, I figured you'd be a little longer, and I really want to get through this blanket before your parents get home. Raincheck, ok?"

Vidia's bright green eyes filled with tears. "But Grandma, you said we'd play cards," her voice trembled as she spoke.

Vidia's reaction surprised her grandmother. "Ok, dear. I guess the baby blanket can wait a little longer." Vidia grabbed the cards and started dealing.

Just then the phone rang.

"That's great news, great news. I'm so happy for the both of you," Grandma said. "Yes, she's right here, one moment." Grandma handed the phone to Vidia.

"Vidia, sweetheart," her dad said.

"We've got news!" her mom interjected. "You're a big sister!"

Vidia's heart raced. "Do I have a little brother?" she asked hopefully.

There was a moment of silence before her dad responded. "You'll find out tomorrow, when we bring the baby home."

"What?!" Vidia screamed. "You've made me wait nine whole months, and now the baby is here and you're still making me wait!" Vidia's frustration boiled over. She could no longer contain herself. She hung up the phone, threw her cards in anger, stomped up the stairs and slammed her bedroom door. She plopped down on her bed and began nervously biting her fingernails. She then took the baby blanket Grandma made for her from the foot of her bed, draped it over her shoulders and rocked back and forth, trying to calm herself. "Even Grandma can't fix this. It better be a boy, it better be a boy," she said as she anxiously swayed, rocking herself to sleep.

CHAPTER 4:

DELLA OCTOBER

The following morning, Vidia awoke and peered out her bedroom window. *Still nothing. Where are they?* she wondered. She paced back and forth, stopping intermittently to bend down and scratch at the snake bite on her ankle. Without thinking, she broke the black scab open, which relieved the itching for a moment and freed the trapped pus, creating a gooey trail that slowly trickled down her foot. Vidia looked down at her ankle and suddenly realized something was wrong. The area around the bite had turned red and was now swollen.

Great, just what I need. Now it's starting to look bad, and Mom will probably get mad at me for breaking the scab open. I can take care of it myself.

She ran down the hall and into the bathroom, soaked a cotton ball in rubbing alcohol, and dabbed at her wound as a stinging sensation coursed through her whole body. *Good. That means it's working*, she thought as she bit her lip and grimaced in pain. Feeling motivated by the burning sensation, she rubbed viciously at the cut on her leg with the cotton ball until her eyes filled with tears at the sensation. "There. All better," she said out loud, pleased with herself.

Vidia walked back to her bedroom and continued to stare out the window in anticipation. It was time. Finally, it was time. Her mom and dad could be home any minute now, and she'd meet the new baby and find out whether it was a boy or girl.

Vidia's thoughts ran wild. *I hope Mom and Dad aren't mad at me for hanging up on them. What if they decide they like the new baby more than me? What if Grandma decides the same? What if the little slug gets more attention than me? Everything is going to be different, I just know it. I'm going to be an afterthought. Will Dad still take me trick-or-treating? This baby has horrible timing. Halloween is so close. What if Mom and Dad are too focused on the new baby to even dress up with me?* Dressing up with her parents was one of Vidia's favorite things to do. *I won't stand for that. I won't let that happen. I'm Mom and Dad's favorite, and I'll make sure that never changes. I'll do whatever it takes.*

Vidia tapped on the window impatiently, trying to unscramble her jumbled angry thoughts.

Am I overreacting? Why does the thought of having

a sibling scare me so much? I can learn to share, and Grandma said having a sibling was great. She paused, now staring into her mirror and trying to collect herself. *What's wrong with me? I should be excited, not filled with all this hatred. I can control this.*

She heard the car pulling into the driveway, and her stomach dropped.

"Vidia, your parents just pulled in!" Grandma exclaimed with excitement from the bottom of the staircase. "Come on down! Let's meet that baby brother or sister of yours!"

Vidia took a deep breath and walked out of her room to the top of the staircase, staring down with narrowed eyes. "I can control this," she repeated to herself.

"Vidia, sweetheart. We missed you," Dad said as he walked into the foyer, looking up at Vidia. Mom smiled, walking in behind Dad, nodding in agreement. "We sure did, big sister."

Vidia could see the car seat in her dad's hand. She took a deep breath and walked down, following her parents and grandmother into the family room.

Mom took the baby out of the carrier. "Meet your baby SISTER! Her name is Della October! The newest addition to the Gardner family! Isn't she beautiful? Would you like to hold her?" Mom said, beaming with the biggest smile Vidia had ever seen.

How can Mom love this baby so much already? She barely knows her. Is this little brat already Mom's favorite? Vidia wondered. She stood motionless without saying a word. Tears welled up in her big green eyes.

"I just knew you'd love her!" Mom said, as she too started crying.

Dad looked on with worry. He was sometimes able to read Vidia better than Mom.

"Do you have anything to say, V?" Dad questioned.

Grandma eyed Frank and then Vidia. "Here, let me take her. I haven't met my new grandbaby yet," she said, sensing the tension and swooping Della up.

Vidia's hands balled up into fists. Her face turned a deep shade of red, and she began visibly trembling. She couldn't contain herself any longer.

"A girl?!? Why did it have to be a girl!?" she screamed. "A boy I could have maybe dealt with, but a snot sucking troll of a girl!! I just can't."

"Vidia, enough," Dad said sternly, putting a hand on Charlotte's shoulder.

"NO. No! No, Dad, that's not enough. I already hate her. Take her back to the hospital right now and tell them you don't want her."

"V. Go to your room."

But Vidia still wasn't done. "My. Name. Is. Vidia," she seethed, gnashing her teeth and standing on the couch to make herself as big as she could. "And you need to change her name. I used it for one of my dolls years ago. This is the worst surprise ever. I hate it."

Mom's happy tears turned sad with despair as she began sobbing quietly. Without saying a word, she took Della from Grandma and left the room.

Realizing that she'd hurt her mother, Vidia felt a slight tinge of confusion and remorse.

"Go to bed now. Don't make me tell you again," Dad said with force, pointing angrily towards the staircase.

"Fine. I don't want to be down here anyway." Vidia jumped off the couch with a loud thump, turned up her nose, and stomped upstairs.

Once back in her room, she pulled her baby blanket close and began rocking back and forth while deep in thought.

Why did they have another baby? Was I not good enough or something? I hate them for doing this to me, and I hate that nasty brat, Della.

Vidia stopped rocking for a moment. *Mom looked so sad. Why does she want me to like the baby so badly?* she wondered.

She started rocking again, and began to wonder why she had such a wild outburst. She resolved to go downstairs and apologize, but just as she was getting up her ankle pulsated with a throbbing, painful itch. She bent down and viciously scratched at it. She scratched and she scratched, unable to satiate herself.

Somewhere in the depths of Vidia's mind, something snapped and every ounce of remorse was obliterated. The light overhead flickered ominously as a cold breeze unexpectedly swirled through Vidia's room.

"It's all over, Vidia my dear. Little Della is Mom

and Dad's favorite now," a hushed, demented voice whispered.

"Who's there?!" a frightened Vidia cried, her teeth chattering in the icy air.

"Only me. You and me. Or should I say you and you? Not to worry, it's just us. Nothing to be afraid of. I'm here to take care of you and fix all of your—well, *our* problems," the voice continued in a depraved, wicked tone. "What's yours is mine," it snarled sarcastically, with a little giggle.

"Go away! I can take care of myself," Vidia stuttered uncomfortably. "I like being alone."

"We are alone. You still don't get it, do you?"

Vidia noticed the air around her mouth cast a vapor into the frigid room. Finally, it dawned on her that she was the one speaking these twisted words and her stomach dropped.

"You're me? I still don't get it."

A smile crept across her face. "You don't have to. Just do as I say. It's easy enough. I'll make everything right again."

CHAPTER 5:

V

Vidia stared into her full-length mirror in her bedroom, posing with her favorite dress on. "I need to look my best," she said to herself with determination. "Grandma and Grandpa will be here any minute. Tonight needs to go well. Everyone will be watching me extra close after the way I acted last night. I can fix this."

The doorbell rang almost on cue.

"Vidia, Grandma and Grandpa are here! Come say hi!" Dad called up the stairs.

"Show time," Vidia said, looking at herself in the mirror. "Time to remind them why I'm the favorite." She was about to turn away and walk downstairs as she caught an eerie grin creeping across her face in the mirror's reflection. She froze and stared back, dumbfounded. The reflection motioned with her pointer finger, gesturing for Vidia to come closer. Vidia shook her head in protest. The reflection then blurred as the mirror was overtaken by frost. Vidia watched as the now shadowy image drew a V into the frost of the mirror. Vidia read the letter out loud. "V?" she questioned. The reflection's grin grew as it nodded and put a finger to its lips. "Shhh." Terrified, Vidia raced out of the room and downstairs.

Vidia walked into the family room, relieved to no longer be alone. Grandma was sitting in a chair holding Della as Grandpa looked on.

"She's adorable. You did great," Grandpa said, looking at Charlotte. "Love the name. Very strong. Thought you might go with Frankie." He chuckled and then turned to Frank. "Let's just hope she doesn't end up looking like you," he said with a loud belly laugh.

"Not so loud, Richard," Grandma whispered to Grandpa. "You'll wake her."

"I will not, dear," Grandpa replied. "Now hand her here, my turn."

Mom and Dad looked on, beaming as Grandpa took Della.

Grandma moved over to the couch as she picked up her knitting set and began working.

Hello? I'm right here, Vidia thought. *Why isn't anyone paying attention to me?* She cleared her throat irritably. "Hi Grandma, hi Grandpa." She put on the biggest fake smile she could.

"Hi, sweetheart, didn't see you come in," Grandpa chuckled. "You're one lucky big sis. Look at this cute little doinker."

"What's a doinker?" Mom asked with a little laugh.

"An adorable little nugget, why of course," Grandpa guffawed.

"Doinker is not a word," Grandma interjected.

"Sure, it is. I've been saying it since Frank was a baby. Frank was a doinker. I'm sure Charlotte was a doinker. And Vidia used to be such a cute doinker when she was little."

Used to be? Vidia thought to herself resentfully.

"He'll never give it up, Mom," Dad said to Grandma, shaking his head. "He's made it a word."

"Isn't Della the cutest little doinker you've ever seen?" Grandpa asked Vidia. Vidia wasn't sure if she was more irritated over Grandpa's rambling or being asked if Della was the cutest baby she'd ever seen.

"*I'm* the cutest doinker I've ever seen," Vidia snapped. *Didn't they notice my dress or my hair?* she wondered to herself.

Nobody noticed, V giggled inside Vidia's head.

"I'm not so sure about that," Grandpa replied. "There's a strict age cutoff to be a doinker, and sadly, you're just too old now. Let's see... what comes after doinker?" Grandpa thought for a moment. "I've got it. Would you like to graduate to doinky?" he asked, quite pleased with himself.

"Um, no thanks. That's ok," Vidia replied flatly, deciding she didn't care for either name.

Grandpa persisted, unaffected by Vidia's lack of enthusiasm. "A doinky is a child between the ages of about 7 and 13. So, you see, Vidia, you're much too old to be a doinker. Then, once you hit 14—"

"Richard, for goodness's sake. Stop making things up," Grandma interrupted, not looking up from her knitting.

"Vidia, honey, come sit with me," Mom said, motioning for Vidia to join her on the couch between her and Grandma.

Finally, some time with Mom. That's more like it, Vidia thought.

Just as Vidia sat down, Della started to cry.

"Maybe Della is not a fan of being called a doinker, either," Grandma laughed.

"Guess I've lost my touch." Grandpa shrugged, handing Della to Mom.

"I think she's just hungry. I'll take her in the other room and feed her," Mom replied.

That little troll. She took Mom from us.

Vidia turned to Grandma. "Want to play some cards?"

"Not now, hon. I need to finish this baby blanket."

"Come on, just one hand?" Vidia persisted.

"Maybe later, after the blanket is done."

"Come on," she whined. "That blanket is taking forever."

"You need to be patient," Grandma replied sternly. "Everything is not all about you. You're old enough to know that."

First Mom and now Grandma? No one has time for me with that baby here, Vidia thought.

"Dad, do you want to play cards?"

"No can do, doinky. Still cooking dinner," Dad replied with a wink.

Nobody wants to hang out with you, V sneered in Vidia's ear.

Vidia swatted at her ear as if shooing a fly away. *That's not true, they're...they're just... busy is all,* Vidia replied, trying to comfort herself. *Go away, V.*

"Want to watch the game with me?" Grandpa offered.

"No thanks, I think I'll go help Mom with Della," Vidia hastily responded, desperate to avoid any further discussion about being a doinky.

"That's more like it!" Grandma said, looking up from her knitting and nodding with approval.

Vidia found Mom sitting on the rocking chair singing Della "Sleep Baby Sleep," a variation of the Spanish lullaby "Duermete Niño." Vidia recognized the song immediately as her favorite lullaby from years ago.

Sleep little baby, sleep baby please,
Or the goblin will come and make such a mess.
Sleep little baby, sleep baby please,
Or the goblin will come and feast on thy flesh.
Sleep little baby, sleep baby please,
Or the goblin will come and take you from me.

That's our song! V screamed hatefully inside Vidia's head.

We have to learn to share. Stop it, Vidia replied, calming herself.

"Darling, don't you know it's rude to sneak up on people? Come look at your sister. She looks so much like you did when you were a brand-new baby," Mom said, beaming at Della.

Surprised that her mom had noticed her enter the room, Vidia quickly joined her.

"I don't see any resemblance," Vidia responded, leaning over her mom staring at her sister, who was now in a peaceful slumber.

"Sure, you do. Look at that nose. Just like yours, only smaller," Mom said, rubbing Vidia's back.

"Maybe a little," Vidia admitted.

"Would you like to hold her?" Mom asked with a hopeful look in her eyes.

"Um, I... I guess so," Vidia stammered, surprised at the question. "But what if I drop her?"

"Oh, don't be silly. I'll be right here with you. I'll show you how," Mom replied, standing up and motioning for Vidia to take her seat on the rocker.

"Cradle her in your arms, and make sure her neck is supported, that's the key. Newborns aren't strong enough to hold their heads up on their own. She's still very wobbly."

Vidia nodded, and Mom gently placed Della in Vidia's arms.

For a moment, everything was perfect. Vidia felt

at ease as she watched Della's chest rise and fall with each peaceful sleeping breath. "She's kind of cute," Vidia said quietly.

"You both are," Mom said, her eyes filling with tears. "Let's move her up to the nursery in a minute and then I can have a look at that snake bite. I want to make sure it's healing alright."

Vidia felt a massive weight fall off her shoulders. She stared up at her mom. *Mom is still thinking about me. She just has two kids to take care of now. Why am I so jealous?*

Just then Della stirred and began crying.

"She'll calm down. Just be patient and keep rocking her," Mom said.

Vidia followed her mother's instruction, rocking Della back and forth, back and forth. Unfortunately, Della didn't calm down. She only cried louder and louder.

Throw her on the floor! Make her shut up! V fumed inside Vidia's head. *She's ruining our time with Mom.*

"Stop it! Stop it!" Vidia snapped at V. As Vidia realized she had spoken these words aloud, Mom quickly grabbed Della out of Vidia's hands.

"That is not how you comfort a baby," Mom said, shaking her head in disappointment.

"No, Mom, I wasn't talking to Della. I'm sorry. Please let me hold her. I can make it better. Let me try again."

"No. Vidia, you need to realize this family is bigger now. Everything isn't all about you anymore. You need to learn to be patient," Mom said sternly as she gently patted Della's bottom, and walked out of the room.

Looks like we're all alone. Look what you did, V mocked.

"I didn't do that. YOU did! Why won't you leave me alone?! You're making everything worse," Vidia said.

You know fully well it's not me making things worse. It's that bratty baby. Everyone's new favorite. Did you see the way Mom was so calm with her while she got mad at us? Della was the one making a scene and screaming. That little brat has got to go.

Vidia scratched at her ankle anxiously. "I don't know. I just want things to be normal again. But how can we do that?"

I've got some thoughts, V retorted.

CHAPTER 6:

VEAL AND A PLAN

"Vidia, dinner time," Dad called.

I'm not hungry, Vidia thought to herself as her mind ran wild with shameful thoughts.

You could take her out on your bike in the middle of the night and ride far, far away. Leave her in a ditch somewhere.

No, that's wrong, V. And besides, Mom and Dad would hear us before we got out the door. We could bring her back to the hospital and say we don't want her? That it was all a big mistake. Some other family could take her.

That's even worse than our first idea, V responded, shaking her head and rolling her eyes.

Vidia paused for a moment. *Mom and Dad would never forgive me if I did something to her,* she concluded.

Don't worry, we'll think of a way. They'll never realize it was us, V assured herself.

"Come on, hon, we're all waiting," Dad said, more loudly this time.

Why should I? All they're going to do is talk about Della and how adorable she is, she thought, making a face.

Just then, Grandma walked into the living room.

"Who are you making faces at, silly? There's nobody in here. We're waiting. Come sit next to me. You didn't think we'd forget about you, did you?" Grandma smiled and motioned for Vidia to follow her.

As Vidia entered the dining room, she was overtaken by the spectacular picture of a feast fit for Thanksgiving. The smell invoked a nostalgia in her she couldn't quite place, but made her feel a warm sense of belonging. She paused for a moment, breathing in the delicious aromas, and admiring the many dishes beautifully presented on the pumpkin patterned tablecloth. Dad's famous mashed potatoes and garlic, a green bean casserole, a colorful salad, and a honey roasted glazed ham glistened in the candlelight. As Vidia scanned over the table again, she noticed sitting adjacent to the ham was a rack of lamb, or possibly an undersized rack of beef. She suddenly became voraciously hungry.

"It looks like a Christmas feast in here," Mom said, looking at Dad. "You really went all out."

"We've got so much to celebrate," Dad responded, pouring Mom a glass of wine.

"Richard, when was the last time you made me a meal like this?" Grandma said with a laugh.

"He definitely gets his cooking from you," Grandpa responded, sitting down at the table. "You should have babies more often, Charlotte," he added, cracking himself up.

Vidia had almost forgotten about all her problems until Grandpa's stupid joke. *What is this? They've never cooked this much for my birthday. Why are they making such a big deal about Della?*

That's because she's their new favorite, V whispered back to Vidia. *If we don't do something quick, they'll put you out with the trash. You're yesterday's news. We both are,* she continued.

Grandpa interrupted Vidia's thoughts. "Is it time to eat?" he asked, glancing over at his son. "I'm famished."

Frank nodded. "Yeah, Dad. Dig in everyone." He put his hand on Charlotte's shoulder and smiled softly. "Look at us. A family of four, after all these years." His face suddenly grew somber, and he drew her close to him and continued in a whisper. "Never would have thought..." he slowly trailed off.

Vidia rolled her eyes and clenched her jaw as her dad continued. "Everything is perfect. Exactly the way it was meant to be."

Perfect now? Seriously? So it wasn't perfect with just me?

Mom leaned in to kiss Dad. Vidia recoiled in disgust and glared at her parents viciously, but neither of them noticed, which furthered Vidia's rage.

"I could get used to this," Mom said with a smile as Dad began to pour drinks for the family.

"Me, too," Grandpa interjected. "Same time tomorrow?" he continued.

"Anytime, Dad, you're always welcome," Frank replied.

Vidia dished herself a heaping scoop of mashed potatoes, a small side of green beans, and a couple thin slices of ham. Then she looked at the rack of beef, eyes wide open. Something about the bloody dish captivated her. She took the three biggest pieces she could find.

"My goodness, this is so tender. You've outdone yourself, son," Grandpa said after taking a bite. "Nice and rare just like I like it, delicious. Is this beef or lamb?"

"It's veal," Dad said proudly. "I wanted to do something different for the occasion. Never cooked it before. Glad it's a hit."

"Veal?" Mom said with a look of surprise. "Don't you find that inhumane? Those poor little babies." She moved her piece back onto the serving platter. "I'll stick with the ham."

"Nonsense. The baby cows are the most delicious. Much more tender," Grandpa disagreed.

"Frank, what were you thinking?" Grandma said, pushing the veal to the side of her plate. "Not the most thoughtful of meats to celebrate the birth of a baby. Wouldn't you say?"

"I didn't really think about it like that," Dad responded apologetically.

"Baby cows?" Vidia questioned.

"Yes," Mom responded. "Some people love it. Others think it's cruel."

Vidia took a bite.

"It's delicious, Dad. I *love* it," she said emphatically, as the bloody drippings dribbled down her mouth.

"See that? Vidia agrees with me," Grandpa said, looking for approval.

"Frank, I've lost my appetite," Mom professed, eyeing Vidia's dirty chin. "I'm sorry. I know you went to so much trouble putting this all together, but I just can't. The thought of those poor helpless little calves kept in such inhumane living conditions and then slaughtered."

Dad looked disappointed. "I'm sorry, Charlotte. I didn't think this one through."

Why is Mom so upset? Vidia wondered. *Ever since Della, everything keeps upsetting Mom. She's so different now. As if things weren't bad enough.*

Vidia decided to move on and focus on dinner. After discovering how much she enjoyed veal, she lost interest in everything else on her plate. She devoured the meat, each bite more delicious than the last. Mouth dripping, she scarfed it down like a wolf who hadn't eaten for days. She picked the bones clean, only looking up to take more veal from the pan. By the time she'd eaten the last piece, the entire bottom half of her face was covered in bloody veal drippings. The crimson color stained her skin so deeply that it was hard to tell her lips apart from the rest of her face. She looked more akin to a wild animal than an eleven-year-old girl. When she realized the veal was all gone, she desperately longed for more. She greedily grabbed the pan by the handles and dumped the leftover drippings on her mashed potatoes. She devoured the mashed potatoes that had turned into a soupy mush, flooded with the bloody drippings. As she was nearly done and licking her plate clean, she looked up for the first time since beginning to eat and realized everyone was watching her.

How long have they been watching me? Vidia wondered.

Who cares? We're the center of attention again. Lap it up, V responded.

But they all look disturbed, don't they?

No, they look scared. V grinned broadly for all to see.

"Hon... are you ok?" Dad questioned.

"We should eat baby cows every night, Dad. Grandpa's right. Wow. They're delicious."

"Not likely. Turns out they weren't a hit after all," Dad responded, looking over at Mom.

"But Grandpa and I love it!" Vidia responded.

"After watching you, I'm not so sure I have much of an appetite for it after all," Grandpa chuckled, looking at Vidia's dirty face.

"Alright, alright already. No more veal," Dad declared, getting up from the table. "Now who wants to help with the dishes?"

"Right behind you, Frank," Grandma said, following her son into the kitchen.

"Give me a minute. I'm gonna check the score of the game," Grandpa said, scuttling out of the room.

Mom got up and moved to the now empty seat next to Vidia. "Vidia, what's gotten into you? You're acting up more and more lately. What was that I just witnessed? Where are your manners? I've never seen anyone eat like that in my entire life," Mom said with concern in her voice.

"She's judging us," V whispered.

"What's that?" Mom asked, unable to entirely hear her daughter.

Surprised that she'd said that out loud, Vidia quickly responded. "I was really hungry. What's the big deal?"

"The big deal is you just made a spectacle of yourself, and it was gross. I know you're having a hard time adjusting to Della being here, but this needs to stop. Okay?"

"Fine," Vidia said through gritted teeth.

"Do you understand what I'm saying? Fine isn't an appropriate response," Mom said sternly. Before Vidia could respond, Della started crying. "I need to feed your sister, but this conversation isn't over." With that, Mom left the room.

How dare she, V seethed. *We finally start getting attention again, and Mom has a problem with it.* She kicked her feet out angrily in protest. The festering snake bite brushed against one of the table legs, and a throbbing pain coursed through her body. *Great, we've opened it back up. Now it's really going to get infected, if it wasn't already. This wouldn't have happened if you hadn't gotten so angry. We need to tell Mom about it now.*

Hello?! We've got bigger problems! V responded dismissively. *Don't tell them about your silly little snake bite. If you do, you'll end up at the doctor, or worse, the hospital, and miss out on Halloween.*

That's true, Vidia agreed. *This snakebite will go away eventually, but our problems with this baby never will.* Vidia pondered. *Mom's really unhappy with us. But what's the big deal about eating baby cows? She was acting so weird at dinner.*

A chill swept over the room. *I know exactly what to do and so do you,* V hissed and laughed a low, demented laugh.

Vidia visibly recoiled in shock as V's thoughts entered her mind. *That's too far. We can't.*

V persisted. *No one would ever know it was us. And don't worry. I'll do the dirty work. The only thing you have to do is give me permission. Let me take over,* V said in a more soothing tone.

Vidia shook her head in protest, but V continued dismissing Vidia's reservations. *We'll fool everyone into thinking you're happy. You must behave as if you've grown to like the little troll. Then when everyone thinks things are better, we'll strike.* A sick smile crept across her face. *Isn't this just the yummiest of plans?* V asked with a little laugh.

Vidia bit at her nails anxiously as she thought about V's proposal, and for a fleeting moment, shook herself free of the envy clouding her mind and thought clearly. *You're insane. I won't do it.*

Look. We've been through this before, you stupid girl. It's the only way, V snapped, growing impatient.

Just then, Vidia heard Della's high-pitched scream, causing her anxiety to be replaced with irritability. *I can't handle listening to that for the rest of my life!*

Dad bolted from the kitchen through the dining room and up the stairs to find Della without even acknowledging Vidia. *He didn't even see me. It's like I don't exist.* Vidia's irritability bubbled over into rage, and a darkness filled her. A deranged smirk slowly crept across her still bloody face.

I know what you're thinking, V whispered and cackled with delight.

CHAPTER 7:

THE PUMPKIN PATCH

Vidia paced back and forth in the foyer, anxiously awaiting the arrival of Aurelia.

Finally, something for me. She twirled her witch's hat over and over in her hands as she tried to decide whether she was going to wear it. *What's taking so long?! If she's not here in the next five minutes, I'll just walk over to her house and get her myself.*

Vidia's thoughts drifted back to the day's planned activity.

I hope the farm still has lots of pumpkins and all the best ones haven't already been taken. She decided the hat was a yes, and carefully placed it on her head.

We're going too late this year, V complained.

At least we're still going, Vidia retorted.

Every October, Vidia's family went to their favorite farm to pick pumpkins for Halloween. It was one of Vidia's favorite seasonal activities. Over the last several years, Vidia brought her friend Aurelia. It wasn't always fun hanging out with such a goody-goody, Vidia thought, but she was her only friend. During every Sunday school session, Aurelia was the only kid constantly raising her hand to ask questions and prolonging class. Definitely the teacher's favorite. Vidia would try to pass her notes, but Aurelia would never play along, shaking her head with disapproval. "Not now," she'd always write back.

Still, their trips to the pumpkin patch had yet to disappoint. Although Vidia found Aurelia annoying at times, she did enjoy her agreeable personality and sweet disposition, as it allowed Vidia to easily take the lead whenever they were together. Aurelia happily played the supporting character in all they did.

While Aurelia was generally passive when it came to fun and games, she could not have been more assertive when she believed someone was being mistreated. Aurelia never hesitated to stand up for anyone and anything she believed in. In fact, she even stood up for Vidia on a couple occasions. One time in particular, Aurelia stared down the biggest, meanest kid in class, who probably would have punched Vidia in the face if Aurelia hadn't been there to outwit the dumb boy. This bewildered Vidia, who simply viewed Aurelia as meek. She couldn't wrap her head around the idea that someone so uninterested in the spotlight and quietly composed could also be brave and strong.

In addition to her kindness, integrity and bravery, Aurelia also had quite the imagination. Games were always more fun with her. While Vidia was able to use these admirable qualities to her advantage, she was often downright jealous. Her parents constantly talked about what a wonderful influence a girl like Aurelia was on Vidia.

After pacing impatiently for what seemed like an eternity, Vidia finally heard footsteps on the front porch. Before Aurelia could even knock, Vidia abruptly opened the door.

Aurelia stood there, smiling, and stretched out her arms. Her curly brown hair covered her face. "Brains! Brainnnnsss, I'm so hungry for brains," she croaked, stumbling over the threshold and adjusting her big glasses which had slipped down her nose.

Awkward and clumsy as always, Vidia thought as she caught Aurelia's skinny arm to keep her from falling.

She pulled herself back up and pushed her hair away from her face. Aurelia was lanky and gawky, towering over Vidia, but her face still had a sweetness and childishness about it. She smiled excitedly, showing her high cheekbones and dimples. Her amber eyes sparkled with excitement. "Thanks for that save! Hi! Cool hat, so festive. Where's the baby?" Aurelia said, speaking a mile a minute.

Vidia's heart sank. *Now that brat Della is going to take my friend away, too.*

Almost as if she sensed Vidia's disappointment, Aurelia quickly changed the subject.

"You ready to pick some pumpkins? I'm so excited. Are you getting a huge one like last year? Remember how your dad could barely carry it?" she laughed.

"I'm not sure. I'm a little worried there might not be any good ones left," Vidia replied, happy the conversation had moved on from her sister.

"No way! The best time to go is near the end of the season. That gives the pumpkins the most time to grow."

"Really?" Vidia questioned.

"No clue. But it makes sense to me," Aurelia quipped cheerfully.

"You girls ready to go?" Dad asked, entering the foyer. Aurelia nodded enthusiastically.

"Finally!" Vidia responded, clearly annoyed.

"Alright. Let's go out and wait for Mom in the Jeep. She'll be right down after she's done changing Della."

"Seriously? Again? Why does Mom always take forever now that the baby is here?"

"Vidia. You're old enough to understand that babies are a lot of work. Things are going to take more time now. That's life."

Vidia rolled her eyes and stared sharply at her father, but joined him and Aurelia as they walked outside and climbed in the Jeep. Vidia sat in her seat, silently fuming.

Sensing the tension, Aurelia changed the subject once again. "Mr. Frank, my abuelita wanted me to ask if we could bring dinner tonight and celebrate the birth of Della." She paused and then continued as if she was reading from a card. "Family is such a blessing."

Vidia clenched her teeth, trying to contain her disgust.

"That's really nice. That would be great," Dad replied.

"What's that?" Mom asked as she walked up to the car and put Della into her car seat.

"Mrs. Santiago wants to bring dinner over tonight," Dad answered. "Isn't that thoughtful?"

Mom grinned as she looked up at Aurelia. "We would love that, sweetheart."

Speak for yourself! V hissed to Vidia.

The drive to the farm passed quickly. Vidia's sour mood lifted, and the girls both chatted excitedly the entire time, alternating between quiet whispers and loud outbursts. They were clearly hatching some sort of plan for the weekend, which tickled Frank and Charlotte. It was so good to see their daughter acting like a normal preteen again. When the girls asked about having a sleepover on Halloween night, complete with a horror movie marathon, creepy stories, and all their favorite snacks, Frank and Charlotte were more than happy to say yes—as long as Aurelia's grandmother was okay with it.

Vidia and Aurelia did not have much of a social life and hadn't yet been invited to a sleepover, so the prospect of their own was thrilling. Vidia struggled to get along with most children due to her controlling tendencies, and her bad temper didn't help the matter. On the other hand, Aurelia was teased for being a goody two-shoes and her grandmother kept her very sheltered. They both agreed their slumber party would be the start of another great Halloween tradition, but Aurelia was a little worried her grandmother might not approve.

"What a pretty drive. This time of year is my very favorite," Aurelia commented as she stared out the window. Although Vidia usually found Aurelia's positivity obnoxious, this time she couldn't help but agree. Their ride was a scenic one, painted with bright splatterings of red, orange, yellow, and brown along the way.

The farm was nestled in a rolling, secluded valley, tucked deep away in the woods. They only passed the occasional house, stopping once along the way for several loose chickens sauntering slowly across the road. Vidia's dad waited patiently as a young boy about her own age ran out into the road to herd the chickens back to safety, smiling and waving to Dad as if to say thank you. The boy seemed so happy, Vidia thought. She wondered what it would be like to live out in the country, surrounded by more animals than people. Did that little boy consider those chickens his pets, or were they just food? Either way,

Vidia decided it was pretty cool. Much to her disappointment, she didn't even have a pet. A black cat was at the very top of her Christmas list every year.

They pulled down a bumpy dirty road, which Vidia recognized from the previous years and knew they were about to arrive.

"This is one rough road. You'd think they would pave it," Mom said. Within seconds of her comment the car hit a deep pothole, causing Della to wake up and fuss.

"One of the many reasons we drive Jeeps," Dad said in a goofy tone, patting the front driver's side dashboard. "It's hardly noticeable."

"True, but that last pothole was bad. We don't want to upset Della right before we get out of the car," Mom replied.

"Where's the fun in that?" Dad questioned. Sensing Mom's building annoyance, he quickly added "Roger. No more potholes." He slowed down and drove carefully as they pulled into the grass field used as a parking area.

Vidia jumped out of the car and paused for a moment to take in the sights and sounds. The air had a crisp, cool breeze that chilled her to the bones since she refused to wear a coat. Each gust of wind caused a flurry of leaves to separate from their branches and wildly swirl throughout the air, floating to the ground only to be picked up moments later by the next gust of wind where they whirled around with the newest batch of fallen leaves.

This is perfect, Vidia thought. *Maybe Halloween will still be fun after all.* She danced with excitement, enjoying the sensation of crunching leaves beneath her feet.

"Looks like it might storm," Mom said, staring up at the clouds forming overhead as the leaves continued to wildly flutter around them.

"Hmm, it does. I didn't think it was supposed to rain until tomorrow. We better get moving," Dad responded.

"Would you like to push the stroller?" Dad asked, looking at Vidia.

"Um. Can't you or Mom do it?" Vidia mumbled.

"I can!" Aurelia interjected eagerly.

"Actually, sure, Dad. I will," Vidia responded quickly, unable to tolerate the enthusiasm on Aurelia's face.

"She's so cute. I always wanted a brother or sister. You must be so happy," Aurelia said, peering over the stroller at the sleeping baby.

If Vidia had paid attention to her friend, she would have noticed the tears welling up in the corners of her eyes as she longingly stared at Della, realizing she would never have any siblings.

"You're so lucky," she continued, wiping her eyes.

Lucky? Vidia thought bitterly. *How could some annoying baby who cries all day and takes all of Mom and Dad's attention away from me possibly make me lucky?* Vidia then noticed her friend's watery eyes and had a fleeting moment of sympathy. "She is kind of cute. Being an only child has its perks too, though."

"Wow, look at that," Mom said, pointing to an enormous black pumpkin cauldron overflowing with purple steam at the entrance to the pumpkin patch.

"How spooky," Dad said in a silly tone, standing next to the life-size witch figurine that peered out from behind the cauldron. He held his hands up in claw form, stuck his tongue out and mimicked the witch's scary face. Vidia surprised herself by laughing out loud at her father. Lately, she hadn't found his jokes funny at all.

Vidia decided a minute of pushing the stroller was more than enough help. "Mom, can you push Della now?"

"Sure, hon. Go have some fun," Mom said.

Vidia walked up to the witch's cauldron and ran her fingers through the purple vapor, wondering how the steam was created. She then waved her hands overtop the cauldron as if she was casting a spell and sang.

"It's the creepiest time of year,
full of nasty fun and fear!
This evil witch is ready to play,
and if you say no, I'll end your day!"

Dad clapped with approval.

"Encore, encore," Aurelia said with a laugh, handing Vidia a broom that was propped up against the cauldron.

Lifting the broom high over her head and relishing the attention, Vidia continued her song.

"In the darkest dark of the night,
this wicked witch is high in flight.
Run in terror, run in fright—
there's no escaping me tonight!
I'll start with your toes
and end with your nose.
What a delicious, meaty meal—
Even better than newborn veal!"

"Run, run!" Aurelia laughed as she ran into the pumpkin patch. Vidia joined her, chasing close behind as she sang her song. The girls played for several minutes while they scoped out all the different pumpkins.

"You girls ready to pick your pumpkins?" asked Dad as Vidia and Aurelia made their way back.

"I found the perfect one. It's just over the hill," Vidia replied, motioning for everyone to follow her.

"Great. Would you like to pick one for Della, too?" Mom asked, following after Vidia.

"So I can pick two pumpkins this year?" Vidia questioned with excitement.

"Of course. Pick one you'd think your sister would like," Mom responded.

"Two pumpkins this year?" Aurelia laughed. "I told you that you were lucky to have a sibling."

"That's a big one," Dad said, looking over Vidia's pumpkin. "You sure you don't want one that's a little smaller? Remember how hard a time you had carving that behemoth last year?"

"Nope, this is the one, Dad. Don't worry, you don't need to carry it this time. There's a wagon right here for us!" Vidia hoisted up her pumpkin, and after a bit of a struggle managed to awkwardly place it in the wagon. "Can you pull it, though?"

Dad laughed. "Not a problem."

"Ok, what about the one for your sister?" Mom asked.

Vidia beamed. "I'll find one for Della now." She excitedly ran full speed ahead, up and over another hill. *Finally, something that's actually good about Della*, she thought. *I've always wanted to get one of those white ghost pumpkins, but I could never go without the classic orange pumpkin. This is perfect. Now I can get one of each!* Vidia's green eyes sparkled with delight. She found a medium-sized, perfectly round ghost pumpkin and added it to the wagon.

"Della and I are all set," she proclaimed.

"Me, too," Aurelia said, placing hers in the wagon as well and giving it a silly little pat of approval.

"So are we. Let's get this show on the road before the storm," Dad said, placing two more pumpkins in the wagon.

As they were standing in line at checkout, Della awoke and started crying.

"Can I please hold her? Please?" Aurelia begged.

"Okay. You have to be very careful with her. She's still so tiny," Mom said, taking Della out of her stroller and handing her to Aurelia. Try as she might, Aurelia was unable to soothe Della. Her cries became more and more urgent.

"Here, you try," Aurelia said, handing Della to Vidia. "Maybe she wants her big sister."

Before Vidia could find a way to reject the proposal, Aurelia had passed Della to her.

Vidia awkwardly but instinctively swayed back and forth and patted Della's back. Within seconds, Della stopped crying.

"Look at that!" Mom said, beaming.

"Looks like you've got the magic touch," Dad agreed.

"I knew she wanted her sister. What little baby wouldn't?" Aurelia said, pleased with her diagnosis.

Vidia didn't know what to think and was puzzled that she was able to soothe the squirming pink little blob. "She... likes me?" she questioned, thinking out loud.

"Oh, my goodness, of course she does!" Mom said, surprised with Vidia's sudden timidity.

A wave of emotion overtook Vidia as she looked down at her sister, who stared up at her, innocent and wide-eyed. Vidia's cold heart started to melt, and she felt a strange warmth inside. *Could this be affection I'm feeling? Maybe it's not so bad having a sister after all.* Vidia snuggled her head into her sister. "You can go back to sleep, little Della. There's nothing to be afraid of, Vidia's got you," she said in a soothing tone.

Sensing all eyes on Della instead of her, the anger inside boiled over, and the moment was lost. Her eyes flashed with jealousy, and she pulled Della closer to her as she whispered, "So long as you don't get in my way."

CHAPTER 8:

A VULTURE DESCENDS

Dinner was always a hit when Mrs. Santiago brought food over, and this time was no exception. Her home-made pizza was the perfect way to end the day at the pumpkin patch.

"Can I please go trick-or-treating with Vidia to-morrow and have a sleepover at her house? Please?" Aurelia begged her grandmother in between bites of the pizza.

"I don't see why not, so long as Mr. and Mrs. Gard-ner are okay with it," Mrs. Santiago responded with a thick accent and a wise, weathered voice.

Mrs. Santiago was a short, stout old lady, with dark, twinkling almond-shaped eyes and a square jawline that softened when she smiled. Her wrinkly face looked very austere, yet still had a kindness about it. Most people were surprised to find out Mrs. Santiago was Aurelia's grandmother, as Aurelia already towered over the little old lady at the age of eleven. The only features she shared with her grandmother were her almond-shaped eyes and brown, curly hair, although her Abuela's hair was now peppered with gray.

"Mom and Dad already said yes. This will be so much fun," Vidia said with excitement.

"We did indeed, Aurelia is always welcome. We'd love for her to join us," said Mom, looking at Mrs. Santiago.

"Absolutely, Aurelia is family," Dad said, with a mouth full of his sixth piece of pizza. "This is delicious. Thanks for adding the anchovies to one side. Nobody likes them but me!" He chuckled and Vidia made a fake gagging noise from across the table.

"I am partial to them too, but the children never seem to like it." Mrs. Santiago eyed Vidia and continued. "Aurelia, you can go to the sleepover, but I don't want you staying up too late," Mrs. Santiago said.

Aurelia clasped her hands together with excitement. "Thank you, thank you!"

Vidia smiled with approval, but her face quickly contorted to a grimace as V made her presence known. *What were you smiling about? You stupid girl. Did you not hear Dad talking about your friend being FAMILY? Our family is already too big as it is. Do you remember when everything was all about you? Those were the days.*

"Thanks again for dinner, Mrs. Santiago. It was delicious," Dad said, wiping his face.

"Not a problem," Mrs. Santiago replied, getting up from the table and starting to collect the dirty plates.

"You don't have to do that. Please sit. You've already done more than enough," Mom said in protest.

"It's no trouble at all. Besides, I've got a little helper," Mrs. Santiago said, eyeing Aurelia.

With that, Aurelia was up and collecting the plates along with her abuela and Mr. Gardner.

"You'll likely have your hands full momentarily anyway. I suspect that little one is about to start crying," Mrs. Santiago said.

Within seconds, Della started wailing.

How does she do that? Vidia wondered.

Mrs. Santiago never explicitly said so, but she always seemed to know what was going to happen ahead of time. Vidia and Aurelia were both convinced she had some sort of sixth sense. Late at night when Aurelia was settling for bed, she would sometimes hear her abuela talking in the other room. Although nobody was ever there, Aurelia was convinced she was speaking to someone and wondered if it could be her parents. She hoped maybe it was. When Aurelia relayed these occurrences to Vidia, her friend was skeptical and quick to point out that Mrs. Santiago was probably just a crazy old lady. Aurelia disagreed and prayed every night that she'd one day inherit her grandmother's sixth sense. She hoped desperately that it ran in the family. She would have given anything to talk to her mom and dad, to put voices to her beloved pictures of her parents that she kept on her nightstand. Her greatest fear was that as time passed, the few memories she had of them would slowly escape her entirely. Even if her grandmother was simply a "crazy old lady" talking to herself, Aurelia found comfort in the thought that there was a chance it was something more. She'd asked her grandmother what she was doing several times, but her answer was always the same. "Shh, quiet mija, you know not to interrupt me when I'm in prayer."

Vidia found Mrs. Santiago very off-putting. There was just something about her gaze she couldn't stand, something that seemed to pierce through any lie or attempt at manipulation. Vidia felt that Mrs. Santiago was particularly hard on her. Vidia was usually able to get away with whatever she wanted and was convinced it was because she was so smart and charming. Mrs. Santiago's ability to see through Vidia's tricks was a blow to her ego and made her dislike Mrs. Santiago intensely.

"Vidia, go help with the dishes. Everyone is cleaning but you. Our guests shouldn't be doing all the work," Mom said, as she began to feed Della.

"I'm finishing my drink, and besides, you're not helping," Vidia responded angrily.

"Excuse you. You better not be talking back to your mother," Dad said as he re-entered the room and swooped up the dirty pizza pans from the table.

Vidia glared up at her father and then back at Della. *Greedy, fat baby pig,* V snarled in her head. "Della eats too much. Mom just fed her forty-five minutes ago," Vidia declared, very sure of herself.

Mom let out an exhausted sigh. "You sure have a lot to learn about babies, Vidia."

Dad handed Vidia the pan and gestured toward the kitchen. Realizing her parents weren't going to change their minds, she reluctantly went into the kitchen to help with the rest of the cleanup.

Much to Vidia's surprise, the cleanup went quickly. *It still would have been quicker if Mom helped like she used to before Della,* she thought, rolling her eyes to herself.

"So can we carve our pumpkins now?" Vidia asked, trying to sound cheerful and hoping everyone had forgotten about her attitude.

"You got it," Dad said. "I'll set the table up out back and start on the campfire. Girls, can you carry the pumpkins around to the patio?"

Vidia and Aurelia ran out to the car and brought the pumpkins around the house and to the backyard patio. Everyone gathered at the picnic table as Dad worked on the fire. In the Gardner household, pumpkin carving was not complete without a campfire. This family tradition was one that Vidia very much looked forward to every year. Her eyes twinkled with excitement as she watched Dad get the fire set.

"Do you need any help?" Aurelia asked.

Ugh. Why does she always want to help? It's just to *make me look bad.* Vidia glared as Aurelia got up to follow after Frank.

"Uh, sure. The wood is a little wet from the thunderstorm. Can you gather more kindling for me? That should do the trick, and we'll be able to get the fire going. Thanks," Dad replied, more accustomed to Vidia's attitude lately and almost taken aback at such courtesy. Aurelia nodded her head and began to collect the kindling.

Once the fire was lit, Dad turned to Mrs. Santiago. "We've got an extra pumpkin. Would you like to carve it?"

Before Mrs. Santiago could respond, Vidia piped up. "We don't have any extras."

"Della's too young to carve her pumpkin, silly. It's Mrs. Santiago's if she's interested."

Mrs. Santiago thought for a moment. "Sure, why not. It's been a while since I carved one." She smiled.

Vidia fumed. *That was my second pumpkin. I picked it out! Now I have to give it to this creepy old lady? She's way too old to even carve a pumpkin.*

Mrs. Santiago turned to Vidia. "So long as you're okay with it?" she asked.

Vidia was convinced she could see the slightest bit of a smirk on Mrs. Santiago's face as she asked the question. Vidia's anger turned to fury. *Look at her, taunting me in front of everyone. How dare she!*

V responded to Vidia calmly. *Don't worry, my dear. We'll get her back, just you wait. But for now, you need to remain calm if you want to have a fun Halloween.* Vidia took a deep breath and replied, her voice shaking with controlled rage. "Of course, Mrs. Santiago." She bolstered a fake smile and focused on her pumpkin.

Mom put on her favorite spooky Halloween music, and everyone started carving their pumpkins in the setting sun. Dad made the same big-nosed, small-eyed Quasimodo that he did every year. Vidia found it ugly as ever, but Dad always looked so pleased with himself. Mom's pumpkins, on the other hand, always impressed Vidia. Last year she'd carved an ornate owl, using a razor on each feather to create a beautiful look when illuminated. This year, Mom sloppily carved an eight-legged spider as she periodically checked on Della.

Mom can't even carve a pumpkin anymore now that she's had a baby? There's no excuse for that pathetic pumpkin. Della has been asleep the entire time.

"Geez Mom," Vidia couldn't help but remark once she saw her finished work. "I think Dad's is actually better than yours this year."

Both her parents laughed, and it was clear to Vidia that her mom couldn't have cared less. Vidia had been hoping to offend her. *This baby is still ruining everything, and she's not even here with us right now!*

Just then, Della began crying. Mom raced inside. *As if this is some sort of tragedy. She's always crying,* Vidia thought again sarcastically. Mom brought Della outside and sat back down at the picnic table, this time closer to the fire, and rocked her back and forth. Everyone seemed to forget they were carving pumpkins and instead began doting on Della and how adorable she was. Vidia remained silent throughout the conversation, seething to herself as she continued to carve her pumpkin. After several minutes, Vidia reached over and squeezed Della's cheeks with her thumb and forefinger. Della looked up at her, wide-eyed and innocent, and Vidia stared back at her with her green eyes narrowed and a closed-mouth smile.

"Vidia, that's too rough. Take your fingers off her face," Mom said, concerned.

"I can't help it, Mom. Her cheeks are so cute. I could just squeeze her to death." Vidia's tone was chipper but her eyes opened wide and sparkled maliciously in the reflection of the fire as she spoke.

"You're not listening. Stop it right now."

Realizing her façade was starting to slip, she released her sister's face from her grasp. "You know, people squeeze babies' cheeks all the time, Mom, especially when babies are super cute like her." She looked her sister over as if doting on her and noticed Della's face had red splotches on both cheeks that glistened, wet from Vidia's pumpkin-gut covered fingers. A little smirk spread across Vidia's face, and she quickly looked up and around, hoping she hadn't given herself away.

"I'm all done. Check it out," Aurelia said, holding her pumpkin up for everyone to see. Its downward slanted eyes were topped with big, broad eyebrows. The wide mouth was agape with several sharp-looking teeth carved into it. Its little button nose was barely visible. She hoped for a happy, silly-looking jack o' lantern, but what she created had a weird look about it and a scary, menacing smile. Aurelia laughed at her unintentionally creepy pumpkin and decided she liked it.

Staying true to her theme this year, Vidia carved the silhouette of a witch. Her carving had a large pointy hat, long crooked nose, hairy chin, and a skinny neck. The silhouette had hands outstretched at a downward angle, as if the wicked witch was about to pounce on her prey just below her fat fingers and out of view.

"That's cool! She looks like she's about to eat someone," Aurelia said, eyeing Vidia's work. Her friend's speculation pleased her immensely.

Mrs. Santiago took the pumpkin carving very seriously, much to everyone's surprise. While everyone else had finished their pumpkins, Mrs. Santiago was nowhere near done. "Do you happen to have any paint?" she asked, staring at her work with intensely focused eyes.

"I can look for some that might work," Mom offered. "We might just have watercolors though." She walked back into the house with Della and was gone for several minutes. She came back with an acrylic paint set Vidia immediately recognized as a birthday present from a couple of years ago.

"Did I say she could use that?" Vidia muttered, further angered by the old lady.

Mom placed the paint next to Mrs. Santiago, walked over to Vidia and sat down at the edge of the table beside her. She spoke to her in a hushed tone. "Vidia, you were given that paint over two years ago and never even touched it. I'm so sick of this bratty attitude. You're not three years old. If this doesn't stop, no trick-or-treating this year."

Vidia was rendered speechless. She had never been called bratty by her mother before, and the thought of missing out on Halloween was devastating. *You see, all your worries about Della ruining your life are coming true,* V spewed viciously into Vidia's ear. *Mom is ready to cancel our Halloween, all over you letting her know that paint belonged to you!*

Vidia tried to block out V, but these words rang too true for her to ignore. *Mom is such a lazy loaf now,* Vidia thought. *I bet she just wants to go to bed early to be with Della on Halloween so she's blaming me as an excuse.*

"Wow, these all look great! I might need to try something a little different next year," Dad commented, reviewing everyone's finished product and realizing his was the least impressive. "Let's light these bad boys up."

Vidia, Aurelia, Mom, and Dad all walked to the front porch with each of their pumpkins, and Dad lit them one by one.

"They're all scary this year," Mom observed after Dad lit the last one. "Very impressive, everyone."

"Espérame! Don't forget about me." Mrs. Santiago turned the corner from the backyard, holding her pumpkin ever so carefully so as not to smear the wet paint that covered it. She placed her pumpkin on the highest porch step and put the remaining candle inside.

"Go on and light it already!" She gestured towards Frank, excited to see her finished product.

As Dad lit the candle, the light danced through the carved opening to reveal a stunning skull. Two large gaping eyes stared back at its audience with a small cross carved just above and in between them. A broad, smiling mouth swept across the base of the pumpkin, with an upside-down heart-shaped nose squarely in the middle. Black hair was painted onto the top of the pumpkin, and a crimson rose was pictured just above the hairline. The contrast of the black, red, orange, and yellow glow created a striking portrait against the white pumpkin that somehow felt ethereal and lifelike at the same time.

Vidia stared back at it, mesmerized. She was overwhelmed with its beauty, and the yellow glow seemed to heighten the experience. It invoked a host of emotions in her: sadness, fear, longing. She had never before seen a pumpkin so beautiful.

"Do you like my pumpkin?" Mrs. Santiago asked.

"It's amazing," Mom responded. "I forgot how talented an artist you were. I mean, are," she corrected herself as she stared into the flames.

"Now, that's impressive," Dad agreed. "It's interesting, though, that it's burning so much brighter than the others. He paused and bent down, looking intently at the pumpkin. "Huh. You really know what you're doing, Mrs. Santiago."

"Very cool, Abuela." Aurelia grinned, stepping closer to her grandmother and pulling her arms to her chest as she shivered. "I've never seen you make a pumpkin like that," she said, her teeth chattering in the suddenly cold evening air.

Mrs. Santiago put an arm around her granddaughter and peered back and forth between Aurelia and the pumpkin. "Can you feel that chill, mija? What a peculiar night this has turned into." She then turned to Vidia and smiled softly. "Thank you for letting me use your, what did you call it? Ghost pumpkin? It is perfect to make a calavera."

"What's a calavera?" Vidia asked, too entranced by the pumpkin to be bothered by the cold.

"Calavera means 'skull' in Spanish. They are a big part of the Day of the Dead celebrations," Aurelia responded.

"Sí, that is correct, and do you know who is pictured in my calavera?" she questioned, looking at Vidia.

"A dead lady?" Vidia guessed, still captivated by the glowing pumpkin.

"Not just any dead woman, that is Mictecacihuatl. More commonly known as the Lady of the Dead."

"Who is she?" Despite wanting to appear aloof

towards Mrs. Santiago, Vidia's interest was evident at this point.

"According to myth, she rules the afterlife with her husband, Miclantecuhtl. She collects the bones of the dead."

"So, she's like the Devil's wife? Why does she collect bones? How did she get to be ruler of the afterlife?" Vidia asked, her curiosity now on full display.

"Not the Devil. She reigns in the afterlife. This is not heaven or hell. It is an Aztec myth," Mrs. Santiago said seriously. "Little is known about her story, but it is believed that she was sacrificed shortly after her birth when she was still an infant. In the afterlife, she met Miclantecuhtl, and together they now rule."

"That's horrible," Mom said, shaking her head.

Vidia was entranced by the story and confused at her mother's disapproval. "Why is it horrible?"

Mom stared at Vidia, disturbed at her callous reply. "Sacrificing a baby. Who could do that?"

"But then she became queen. Sounds like a sweet deal to me." Vidia felt almost as if she was hypnotized by the grinning pumpkin and the accompanying story.

"Nothing sweet about that story if you ask me," Dad replied. "I'd say it's pretty dark."

"Yes, yes, I agree it's quite the haunting tale, but merely a story. Nothing to worry about," Mrs. Santiago said, putting her hand on Aurelia's shoulder, who looked a bit spooked.

"I should go in and settle Della for the night," Mom said with a yawn. "Thank you for everything. Tonight was wonderful."

"Right behind you, honey," Dad said. He started up the steps after Mom, and then stopped and turned around. "Hang out as long as you want, don't let us spoil the fun. And thanks again for the food." Dad smiled.

"You're quite welcome," Mrs. Santiago responded. "It's getting late for myself, too. These old weary bones, you know." She chuckled. "Thank you for the pumpkin. I have not done that in years. Such a lovely night this has been."

As usual, that boring baby is ruining everything! Vidia thought. She turned to Aurelia hopefully. "So, what do you want to do now?"

"I'm kind of cold and that story about the pumpkin really creeped me out. I think I'm ready to head home. Sorry, Vidia. I'll see you later though! Are you ready, Abuela?"

"Sí, run along. I know you're cold, don't wait up for me. I'll be right behind you," her grandmother responded.

"Today was a blast. Thanks for having me," Aurelia said. "I'll see you bright and early tomorrow," she said with a wink, and waved to her friend excitedly as she ran down the road towards home.

Once Aurelia was out of earshot, Mrs. Santiago fixed her eyes squarely on Vidia. "What is it that troubles you so, Ms. Vidia?" she asked, her eyes narrowing intensely.

Vidia was taken aback. "Nothing," she responded curtly.

"There most certainly is something. I sense such a darkness around you lately. I see the way you look at your sister. Who is it that keeps talking to you in your troubled mind? Speak, child, tell me so I can help you before it's too late."

Vidia's heart began pounding. She hesitated, unsure how to respond. *Should I tell her? This could be a way out.* For a fleeting moment, Vidia imagined the relief of confiding in the old woman. In truth, she hadn't felt very much like herself lately.

You stupid, stupid girl! Your cover is nearly blown. You know you need to keep us a secret in order for me to help you fix things. That old hag doesn't really want to help you, and we don't need anyone, V screamed inside her head.

"I don't know what you're talking about, Mrs. Santiago," Vidia stammered. "You've got me all wrong." She scratched her ankle through her pants as it started burning.

"Alright, young one, I see you won't share. I'm here if you change your mind." Mrs. Santiago looked down at Vidia's pant leg. "Your ankle is infected. What happened?" she demanded with worry in her voice.

"It's just a bug bite," Vidia quickly replied, wondering how Mrs. Santiago could possibly know about the infection. She hadn't even lifted her pant leg to scratch it.

Mrs. Santiago shook her head in disappointment. "We both know that's not true. Please show your mother and have her take care of it. She'll know what to do. You should never let infections fester." With that, Mrs. Santiago turned to leave, but then stopped and looked back at Vidia. She lowered her head in prayer. "'A heart at peace gives life to the body, but envy rots the bones.' —Proverbs 14:30." She bowed her head reverently and continued. "Open your heart to your baby sister, young one, and in turn, you'll find peace."

Vidia stared at her uncomfortably, not sure how to respond. *What a creep*, V sneered disparagingly. Vidia's ankle began to burn yet again and she couldn't stop herself from bending down and grabbing it.

Mrs. Santiago shook her head. "Goodnight, young one." She sighed in disappointment and left.

The flames of the calavera seemed to grow and flicker wildly in the night sky as if it was laughing maniacally, taunting Vidia. She felt a cold chill permeate her body.

She's a witch! Evil, evil sneaky old hag! V whispered to Vidia. *She's trying to trick you into telling her everything, trick you into accepting that little troll.*

But maybe Della isn't that bad. Today was fine, fun for the most part. And she was there too. She didn't really get in the way of anything.

Fine? It used to be great. Mom hardly had time for us today. She was holding Della nearly the whole time.

And even when Dad is with us, he's always checking on Mom and Della. He's not really with us. Not like he used to be.

Vidia watched as the pumpkins glowed bright in the dark night and she suddenly felt a kinship with the flickering, taunting pumpkin that Mrs. Santiago had carved. A strange sensation overcame her and she threw her head back and cackled like a hyena. Vidia danced with delight to the backdrop of the glowing pumpkins.

V hissed with twisted amusement at the scene. *My dearest Vidia, soon to be my vessel. Continue to feed on thine iniquities, and together we will delight in the fruits of our labor. What's yours is mine and what's mine is mine.*

What on earth are you talking about? Vidia laughed. *What's wrong with you? You sound like you're a hundred years old right now!*

Oh, I'm much older than that.

A massive vulture appeared from the darkness of the night, interrupting their conversation. It swooped down in front of Vidia and landed next to Mrs. Santiago's pumpkin. Vidia abruptly stopped dancing and froze. She had seen plenty of vultures throughout her life, but never this big and never anywhere near this close. It was so revolting, so ugly, and something about its face conveyed a depth of wisdom and cunning. The combination made Vidia deeply uncomfortable. Its red wrinkly eyes bore into hers, assessing her, studying her face. Vidia backed away instinctively as the hair on the back of her neck stood on end. The creature spread its wings and cawed loudly with delight. Vidia felt as though the bird was showing off and licking its chops, staring at a helpless, rotting carcass.

Vidia suddenly snapped back to herself. Disgusted with the bird and angry at herself for letting it intimidate her, she screamed into the night, not caring who heard her. "I'm no one's vessel but my own, V! And you, get out of here, you ugly nasty bird!" She lunged forward at the creature, and it promptly flew away.

Rattled through and through, Vidia ran inside, up the stairs and into her room. She threw herself onto her bed and scratched feverishly at her burning ankle.

CHAPTER 9:

Bumps in the Night

Vidia laid in her bed excitedly, staring at her alarm clock and fighting heavy eyes under the comfort of her warm blankets. Finally, her alarm rang out as it struck 1:00 a.m. She smacked the top of the clock, silencing the wake-up call as quickly as possible. Vidia sat up in her bed and held very still for a couple of moments, listening to see if the noise had woken anyone else in the house. She was pleased as all she heard was the sound of herself breathing.

Halloween is finally here! Time for the fun to begin, she thought as she climbed out of her bed and tiptoed across her room to her shoes, careful not to step on any creaky floorboards.

She decided not to waste any time changing out of her pajamas, put on her sneakers, and was ready to go. She started towards her bedroom door and then paused as she recalled the Shadow Box hidden under her bed. A large mischievous grin crept across her face as she pulled out the old, dusty box, imagining Aurelia's scandalized expression at the sight of it. She was sure Aurelia would protest playing with it, but Vidia was still confident she could convince her if she pushed hard enough.

Vidia placed the Shadow Box into her backpack. "Now's the time," she whispered, her excitement nearly boiling over. "Don't chicken out this year, Ellie Ellie Cinderellie."

Last Halloween, Vidia and Aurelia had agreed to sneak into Aurelia's parents' locked bedroom when the clock struck midnight. The girls were sure Mrs. Santiago was hiding something about Aurelia's late parents in that room. Aurelia was desperate to glean more information and was hoping she might find out how they passed away. Ever since her parents died, Mrs. Santiago kept their bedroom door locked.

"It's strictly off limits. There is no debate," she'd say every time Aurelia asked to go in. Some nights, Aurelia could hear the shuffling of feet within the bedroom, and she knew it was her abuela.

"How come she gets to go in there? They're *my* parents!" Aurelia would say indignantly to Vidia. This was the only thing that ever seemed to bother Aurelia about her grandmother, or anyone really for that matter. It was clearly a very raw spot and had been eating at her for a long time. Vidia too was dying of curiosity. However, their first attempt did not go as planned. Vidia waited in the bushes outside Aurelia's house for nearly an hour before she gave up and left. The next day Aurelia claimed her grandmother was still awake so she couldn't let her inside.

What old person isn't asleep at midnight? Vidia wondered, not believing the explanation. *No excuses this year. We're doing it even later.*

Vidia threw her backpack over her shoulder and quickly crept out of the house. The night air had a chill to it, and Vidia relished the biting sensation as she breathed in. There was something about the lonely, empty street that she felt at peace with. The neighborhood road was dimly lit by a few scattered streetlights. She was careful to walk as quickly as possible without looking suspicious.

As Vidia turned the corner to Aurelia's street, a wiry figure clad in all black jumped out at her from behind a tree. Vidia's blood ran cold and she screamed in horror. She attempted to run in the opposite direction and in her panic fell backwards onto the grass. The figure stood over her as she looked up from the ground in terror, and she heard a familiar, joking voice. "Guess who?!"

Vidia's terror melted. "Zach! You jerk! Why would you do that? Someone is going to hear us!"

"C'mon, that was hilarious. I got you good. I didn't know you were such a scaredy cat. And you act like you're so tough." Zach laughed.

"It's called being on alert. There would be something wrong with me if I didn't react. Anyway, you really should watch yourself. I almost punched you in the face."

"Ok, ok, sorry," Zach said, extending his hand to help Vidia, who was still on the ground.

"I don't need your help," Vidia said, still reeling from the incident and angry.

Zach pushed his shaggy, dirty blond hair out of his eyes, and they twinkled with delight as he stood over her. He was always so at ease. Even though he was only eleven years old, he reminded her of a surfer, or what she imagined a surfer to be like. Zach never seemed to take Vidia seriously even when she was infuriated with him, which made her dislike him all the more. Unlike Vidia and Aurelia, he was always surrounded by a bunch of friends when he was outside, playing sports, and riding his bike. Sometimes he'd randomly show up to wherever Vidia and Aurelia were and decide to join in. Both girls were initially surprised he had any interest in hanging out with them, but Aurelia enjoyed his company and quickly warmed up to him over the past couple of months. They were good friends at this point and she considered him part of their group. Vidia, on the other hand, was very hostile and looked at him with suspicion. She couldn't understand why one of the annoying, popular kids would ever want to hang out with a couple of outcasts. She was convinced he was either plotting something or secretly making fun of them behind their backs.

"What are you doing out on the street in the middle of the night anyway?" Vidia demanded as she climbed to her feet.

"I could ask you the same question," said Zach, giving her a sly look.

Vidia pursed her lips together and glared.

"Cat got your tongue?" Zach laughed. "Wouldn't it be funny if we were both headed to the same place?"

Seemingly out of nowhere, a spindly, tall old man wearing a raggedy tweed jacket stepped in front of the children. Zach and Vidia jumped back, both yelling at the same time and falling over each other. The man began laughing wildly, a wheezing, loud laugh that soon turned into a cough. Both children remained on the ground, stunned into silence as they stared at the man. His frizzy, white hair stood out in the moonlight and his outrageously long, bushy eyebrows fell into his bulging eyes, making him look even more crazed. "You should have seen your face, girly. That boy scared you good. And now I've scared the both of you. Stumbling over each other like Tweedledee and Tweedledum." He started laughing again, revealing his rotting, brown teeth. Vidia recoiled in disgust at the sight.

"Do we know you?" she said, trying to sound rude, but clearly frightened.

"No. But I know you, V."

Vidia's stomach lurched, and she stared at the man, trying to figure out whether she had heard him correctly.

"What fun we're all having on this eerie night," he continued cheerfully, clapping his hands and then extending them outwards as he moved toward them. "Let me help you both up. I am sorry for startling you." The old man smiled again, now so close to Zach that Zach could smell his rank breath.

"No, we're fine," Zach said, springing to his feet.

Realizing how uncomfortable his audience was, the old man stepped back before he continued. "Alright, alright. What has the two of you out so early on this dark morning?"

"We don't talk to strangers," Vidia said.

"Leave us alone," Zach added, standing as tall as he could. Vidia was taken aback by the new tone in Zach's voice. She'd never heard him sound so serious ever before.

A large smile crept over the old man's face. "Alright then. I'll leave you two to whatever it is you're up to. Until we meet again. And Happy Halloween!" he said with a flourish and leapt away. Though he appeared quite old, he was surprisingly spry and moved about with a youthful vigor. He bounded down the street, singing to himself. "Ashes, ashes, we all fall down!" He eventually faded into the darkness of the early morning.

Vidia and Zach waited with bated breath, hoping he was gone. After several moments, the darkness of the night was momentarily interrupted as they saw the flickering of a torch's flame in the distance. The children could vaguely make out the silhouette of the crazy old man holding the torch. The man bellowed from a distance cheerfully. "Adios!" His words were followed by a bizarre popping sound neither of the children recognized as both the torch and silhouette immediately disappeared.

"Who was that guy? Such a creep!" Vidia shuddered.

"Definitely a crazy person," Zach agreed. "Who would be walking around at this hour? But anyway, he's gone now. Back to the task at hand. Race you to Aurelia's house!"

"Wait, what?" Vidia protested, but before she could continue, Zach took off running down the street and Vidia bolted after him.

As they reached Aurelia's driveway, Zach bent over to catch his breath.

"Wow, I really had to give that my all. You're pretty fast," he said as Vidia pulled up next to him.

"Or maybe you're just slow." Vidia responded, red with exhaustion and struggling to whisper as she caught her breath.

"Then what does that make you?" Zach retorted.

Vidia couldn't contain herself any longer and raised her voice in agitation. "You had a head start. Tell me what you're doing here already!"

"Quiet, you guys! You're going to wake my abuela," Aurelia whispered frantically, sitting at the bottom of her front porch.

"Oh wow! You didn't chicken out this time," Vidia exclaimed, happy to see Aurelia.

"I told you I'd be here. I would have been last year too if my abuela was asleep. I know you don't believe me, but I need to know what's in that room. More than you, more than anyone!"

"Wait, you did this last year too and I wasn't invited?" Zach questioned jokingly.

"We barely knew you then. And I still don't understand why you're here now," Vidia remarked, her eyes narrowing as she stared at Zach.

"Vidia, don't. I invited him," Aurelia said firmly.

"You could have at least given me a heads up. And all he does is complicate things," Vidia groaned.

"Um, hello? I'm right here," Zach said, amused.

Aurelia cringed. "Come on, guys, stop, or you're going to wake up my grandmother, and then we'll all be in big trouble."

"Fine," Vidia said flatly. She still wanted an explanation and was uncomfortable with Zach's presence, but decided it wasn't worth dwelling on when she was so excited.

Aurelia walked up her porch steps and opened the front door, motioning for Vidia and Zach to follow her. She led them through the kitchen and down a dimly lit hallway.

"That's the room," Aurelia whispered, barely audible but noticeably nervous. She pointed to the closed door.

"It's locked," Zach noted as he tried to turn the handle.

"Good thing we've got you here, Sherlock Holmes," Vidia said, rolling her eyes.

"Yes, she keeps it locked," Aurelia said patiently, ignoring Vidia's jab. "We've got to get the key from my abuela's room." She motioned again to the door on the other end of the hallway. "She keeps it on top of her nightstand."

"Oh no way, I'm not going in there. Your grandma is all kinds of scary," Zach responded, backing away. "And I can't even blame her if she freaks out at some boy in her bedroom in the middle of the night."

For once, Vidia agreed with Zach, but there was no way she was going to let that be known. "Alright, chicken little," Vidia whispered with a smile. "You stay here, and us ladies will go get the key." She tucked her hands under her shoulders and flapped her elbows up and down as she stuck her tongue out at Zach.

"You won't make fun of me when she wakes up and catches you," Zach warned.

Vidia and Aurelia crept up to Mrs. Santiago's bedroom door. Vidia took a deep breath and looked gravely at Aurelia, who nodded at Vidia and motioned for her to continue. Vidia turned the door handle as gently and slowly as she could and pushed.

The moment the door opened, the silence of the night was disturbed by a low rumbling noise that seemed to shake the floor below them. Vidia stepped back, startled by the sound and worried that Mrs. Santiago had awoken. Aurelia gestured for Vidia to come back. "It's fine. That's just her snoring."

"Are you going in and getting the key?" Vidia questioned.

"Aren't you coming with me?" Aurelia asked, her determination beginning to melt as fear took over.

Vidia suddenly felt very nervous too, and shook her head.

"Look who's scared now," Zach whispered as he walked over to the girls. Finding his courage, he took a deep breath and spoke again. "I'll go with you, Aurelia."

Vidia's jealousy overpowered her fear. There was no way she was going to let Zach look like some kind of hero. "No. I'll go!" Vidia blurted out, a little too loudly.

"You guys both go. I'll stay back at the door," Aurelia whispered, sounding relieved. She pushed the door wide open and stepped away.

Vidia and Zach glanced at each other, both determined not to look like chickens, and stepped over the threshold. Their complete inability to work together resulted in a traffic jam. They butted up against each other, shoulder to shoulder, stuck in the door frame. If Aurelia wasn't so scared, she would have laughed hysterically at the preposterous sight.

"I'll go first," Vidia muttered through gritted teeth.

Zach backed off and let Vidia take the lead.

Vidia dropped down to her hands and knees and crawled across the floor. Zach decided to follow suit, keeping close behind her. When she got to the nightstand, Vidia reached up blindly and began feeling around for the key, a little too aggressively. Before she realized what she was doing, she swiped at a glass full of water, knocked it off the nightstand and to the ground. It crashed loudly onto the old wood floor below.

Aurelia gasped in horror from the doorway and covered her mouth. Luckily, Mrs. Santiago's thunderously loud snores masked the noise, and she remained fast asleep. Zach raised his hands and patted the air, as if to say all is well. He then stood up and quickly grabbed Mrs. Santiago's keys from the nightstand. They jingled softly for a split second as Zach quickly clasped his hands around them, silencing the noise. In that same moment, the snores completely ceased, and Zach felt eyes on him. He shifted towards the bed and saw Mrs. Santiago, wide-eyed and staring directly at him. His heart skipped a beat and he froze.

What's he doing? Vidia wondered, still crouched on her hands and knees. She decided she wasn't going to stick around to find out, so she snatched the keys out of his hands and bolted as fast as she could out of Mrs. Santiago's bedroom.

Zach remained motionless, not having taken a single breath since he noticed Mrs. Santiago staring at him. The old woman's eyes seemed to look completely through him, as if he wasn't even there. Zach didn't know what to think. He had only ever seen this expression once on his late great aunt's face when she had passed away. He couldn't shake the feeling he was staring at a corpse.

Zach felt someone grasp his hand and pull him away. He finally came to his senses and ran out of the room, hand in hand with Aurelia.

"Thanks," he said breathlessly to Aurelia once they'd closed the bedroom door and were safely back in the hallway. "I can't believe I froze like that, but your grandma's eyes were wide open and she was staring right at me."

"I'm so sorry. I should have told you my abuela sometimes sleeps with her eyes open."

"Well, that's creepy," said Zach. "She looked like she was dead."

Vidia shivered at the thought of the old woman's almond eyes staring directly at her. "I don't even like when she looks at me while she's awake," said Vidia.

"Alright, alright, I get it, you both think my grandma is scary. Where's the key?" Aurelia asked anxiously. "Please don't tell me we have to go back in there."

"Um, I had it, but then I didn't," Zach said.

"Good thing I was there," Vidia declared, opening her hand to show off the keychain.

CHAPTER 10:

THE SHADOW BOX

Aurelia suppressed an excited squeal and grabbed the keys out of Vidia's hand. She bolted down the hall to her late mother and father's room. The keychain had dozens of similar looking keys on it, but Aurelia knew exactly which one opened the door. This was the moment she had been waiting for nearly her entire life. With bated breath, she inserted the key, turned the knob, and paused momentously.

"Well, get on with it already," Vidia said, breathing down Aurelia's neck impatiently.

"It's just that it's been so long since I've been in their room. I barely remember it. What if it's empty and all their stuff is gone?"

"Only one way to find out," Zach said, trying to sound cheerful.

Aurelia let out a nervous, loud sigh, and pushed the door open.

As she entered the room, Vidia started to follow behind her, but Zach stepped in front of her, effectively blocking her path. "They were her parents. Let's give her a moment."

Vidia rolled her eyes at Zach, but her annoyance quickly faded as she saw Aurelia's eyes welling up with tears. Never one to observe or notice other's feelings without being prompted, Vidia suddenly felt ashamed for not being able to read her best friend as well as Zach.

The bedroom was dank with a strong, musty smell. Even though Mrs. Santiago frequented the room, it was clear that the windows had not been opened in quite some time. As Aurelia surveyed the room she was overwhelmed with a strong sense of déjà vu. Although she loved her abuela dearly, Aurelia always pined for the warmth of her mother and father. For the first time in years, she felt completely comforted and truly at home.

"It's like they're still here," Aurelia whispered, wiping tears away from her eyes. "Everything is exactly how they left it." She walked through the room slowly, looking over everything as it evoked memories that felt like distant dreams. As she stared at her parents' old oak desk, she recalled tugging at her dad's sleeve, urging him to finish up his work for the day. The old blue chair pushed up against the desk had been her favorite way to spin herself dizzy whenever she was bored. Wooden chests lined the walls and most of the open floor. Aurelia remembered jumping from chest to chest, as if playing hopscotch. She never questioned why their room was lined with so many antique chests until now. Rather than rummage through everything, she was now completely uninterested in the opportunity. More than anything, she wanted to be close to her mother and father. She was drawn to the comfort of her parents' bed and climbed onto it, laying down in the middle. She closed her eyes, feeling closer to them than she ever had since they passed away.

"Geez. Pack rats," Vidia said, looking at the maze of wooden chests. "My mom has one just like these hidden in our attic. I wonder what's in them. There's no way we're going to have enough time to go through all of these tonight."

"I don't think I want to anymore," Aurelia responded, now sitting up on the bed, gazing about the room. "Not today, anyway. I'd rather sit here and feel close to them." She noticed a necklace hanging from the corner of the bedpost across from her. "That was Mom's side of the bed," she said, as she moved closer to get a better look. The delicate cross pendant was made of silver and outlined in gold. Everything in the room looked dusty and dingy, but the necklace somehow sparkled in the dim light, as if it had just been polished. A distinct memory of pulling at the necklace on her mother overwhelmed her. She cupped the cross in her hands and tried her hardest to hold back a flood of tears.

"Don't you want to find out why your grandma has been keeping all this from you?" Vidia questioned, disappointed at Aurelia's change of heart.

"Yeah, but not now." She let go of the necklace and sighed heavily.

"We understand," Zach interceded, before Vidia could push the matter any further. He pulled the necklace off the bedpost carefully and handed it to Aurelia. "You should take it."

"I'm not sure my abuela would want me to have it," she said, turning it over in her hands and staring at it longingly.

"She would. They were your parents."

"I think my mom told me I could have this when I was older. That she wanted me to wear it. I'm not sure though. I was so young when they died, so my memories have become so fuzzy and mixed up with my dreams."

Vidia leaned back against the wall, completely uninterested in the conversation. She strummed her fingers and glowered, none too pleased that their investigation was yet again put on hold. She felt something sharp pressing into her back and remembered the Shadow Box in her bookbag.

"I know what we can do. This will help our investigation without disturbing your parents' things." Vidia pulled the Shadow Box out of the bag and bounded onto the bed. She took out the key knife, smiling broadly, and unlocked the box. As she spread it out on the bed, she looked up at Aurelia and Zach, pleased with herself and certain that she already had their full attention.

"What is it?" Aurelia questioned timidly, looking down at the black and gray marble stone.

"It's called a Shadow Box. I think you use it to contact the other side. You know, the spirit world, or something like that. I thought we could have a little fun and try to reach your parents with it. What better way to find out what happened to them than asking them directly?"

Zach shook his head. "The other side? As in ghosts?"

"Yeah, something like that. It says the In Between, whatever that is," said Vidia.

"No way," Zach said with a sense of finality. "This type of stuff only brings trouble. We shouldn't mess with it."

"Oh, please," Vidia countered. "You're just scared. It's exactly what we should be messing with if we want answers." Vidia's remark was met with silence. She waited a beat, and then continued. "Guess you're both too chicken." She spoke theatrically, as if she'd been preparing her lines for this exact moment. "I can't say I'm surprised, Zach." She waved her hand dismissively at him. "You, though." Vidia pointed at Aurelia with a raised eyebrow. "I thought you'd be brave enough. But maybe not, Ellie Ellie Cinderellie?"

Aurelia had been sitting in silence, staring quietly at the Shadow Box during the conversation. She appeared not to be listening at all, when suddenly she piped up, quietly but earnestly. "We could talk to my parents?"

"Yes. I think so. And their old room is the perfect place for it. It's where they spent a lot of time and their belongings are still here. It will make for a strong connection."

"I'll do it," Aurelia responded with conviction in her voice.

Vidia was surprised at the lack of resistance. "Oh goody, this will be perfect," Vidia exclaimed a little too loudly, clasping her hands together excitedly. She untied the deep crimson candles and placed them in the copper candleholders fastened to the box. The candles stood tall, perched upon the upper corners of the wooden panels, solemnly overlooking the marble stone.

"How does it work?" Aurelia asked, moving to get a closer look.

"Not entirely sure, but I think these are the instructions." Vidia pointed to the words etched into the box.

Aurelia squinted to make out the tiny print and read out loud: *"Burn both candles to reach the lost. Ask your questions twice over. Let the flames and the shadows light your path. You never know what may answer from the In Between."* Aurelia glanced at both her friends confusedly. "I don't get it. What does it mean?"

"Trouble, for sure," Zach replied in a defeated tone.

"Ugh, stop spoiling the fun," Vidia countered. "I think it means once we light the candles we can ask our question, and the flames, or shadows or something, will answer us. There's only one way to find out. Do you have any matches so we can light the candles?"

"Um, in the kitchen, but we don't want to go back out there. There's probably some already in here. Abuela has candles everywhere. Check the desk and nightstand drawers," Aurelia suggested.

Zach opened several desk drawers, taking care not to make much noise. "Got 'em."

"Perfect, give them here," Vidia said impatiently.

Zach rolled his eyes. "Not sure why I'm helping with this," he said as he flipped the matches to her. He looked at Aurelia, intent on continuing his objection, but something in her expression stopped him. He'd never seen such a look of longing and sadness on his friend's face and decided against protesting any further.

The matches fell through Vidia's hands, but she quickly grabbed them off the ground where they fell. She pulled one out and then paused thoughtfully. "I bet this will work better with the lights off. Zach?"

"Alright, alright," Zach said as he shook his head and turned the lights off.

Vidia quickly and sloppily lit one of the matches. From the light of the match, two candles on top of the desk caught her eye. The candles were identical, long and skinny, encased in now dusty glass. A picture of a man in a green robe was painted onto the candles and looked as if he was staring directly at Vidia with a very serious expression. He had a blazing orange flame above his head and held a wooden staff in his hand. Vidia wasn't sure why she felt so drawn to the image. "Who is that?" she asked, pointing at the candles.

"That's St. Jude. They're prayer candles. Abuela has them all over the house," Aurelia said. "She has others too, but a lot of St. Jude."

"Why so many of him?" Vidia questioned.

"I don't really know. He's the patron saint of lost causes."

"Ow!" Vidia exclaimed as the match's flame reached her fingers. The match fizzled out and the room went dark.

She struck another and walked over to light one of the candles of St. Jude.

"Wrong candle. Vidia, what are you doing?" Zach asked.

"Why lost causes?" Vidia said, ignoring Zach as the glow from the candle illuminated the old bedroom in an eerie amber hue.

"It's a family thing. I guess it's my abuela's calling or something. I've never really thought much about it," Aurelia responded, motioning for Zach and Vidia to join her back on the bed. "Do you want to keep talking about candles, or are you going to show us how to use this thing?"

Realizing that she'd become sidetracked, Vidia jumped on the bed and landed between Zack and

Aurelia, knocking one of the candles out of its candleholder. Aurelia swiftly placed the candle back in place and eagerly whispered to her friends. "Let's get started!"

Vidia lit another match, this time more carefully. She raised it to one of the crimson candles, and the wick quickly took to the flame, almost as if it jumped toward it before Vidia had a chance to touch the two together. The candle made a loud popping sound and sparked a couple of times. The trio backed up instinctively, startled by the strange noises. The candle then quieted, and a blue flame burnt softly. A dim blueish hue cast a glow onto each of their faces.

"That looks... really odd," Aurelia said.

"It's just super hot," Vidia replied confidently.

"Candles don't get that hot. Not normal candles anyway," Zach whispered.

Vidia smiled broadly and lit the other candle as the same popping sound echoed throughout the room. Again, it sparked several times before it began to burn in the same dark shade of blue.

Aurelia reached her hand up to one of the candles. "It's not hot at all. It's as cold as ice," she said in a hushed voice.

Zach and Vidia followed suit, raising their hands to the blue flames and felt an eerie chill on the tips of their fingers.

"A cold flame. How?" Zach asked.

"It means it's working," Vidia said, still trying to sound confident, but her voice shook. Aurelia and

Vidia huddled closely together, surrounding the Shadow Box.

Zach moved away from the box and crossed his arms uncomfortably, eyeing the two girls. "And my mom thinks my other friends are trouble."

"Now what?" Aurelia eagerly asked.

"We ask our questions," said Vidia, and reached out for Aurelia's hand. She then turned to Zach and reached for his hand, too. Noting his hesitant expression, she continued, "I'm sure it works better with more people."

Zach didn't say a word, but took Vidia's hand in his and then Aurelia's. The three children huddled together tightly around the Shadow Box.

Vidia closed her eyes and spoke in a hushed, somber tone. "Shadow Box, are we alone in this room tonight?"

The blue flames began dancing wildly and grew larger, each one doubling in size and bending forward toward Vidia. An icy chill seemed to ooze out of the candles and envelope the room.

"Can you guys feel that?" Zach whispered through chattering teeth, his breath visible in the frigid air as he spoke.

"Yes," Aurelia said quietly. Although her voice was low and calm, her eyes were now wide with both fear and excitement.

"This is so cool," Vidia whispered, smiling broadly. Her exhilaration was suddenly swept away as her snake bite began throbbing intensely. She doubled over in pain and gritted her teeth to avoid screaming.

Stop it! Stop it right now, you foolish, silly little girl! Don't invite them in when you already have me! V snarled.

Go away V. I'm just having fun with my friends, Vidia replied, trying to remain calm.

"Shadow Box, are we alone in this room tonight?" she repeated, feeling defiant.

The blue flame on the left-hand side of the box jumped off its wick and down onto the black marble stone as if it were alive. It slowly traveled up and down, its flickering fire growing fainter and fainter as it moved, leaving a glowing blue trail in its wake. By the time the flame finished inscribing the letter N on the stone, it had become so small it was now the size of a teardrop. As if the flame knew it was about to flicker out, it jumped back up to its wick where its blaze burned steadily once more. Impatiently waiting, the blue flame on the candle that sat on the right-hand side of the box now took its turn. It darted onto the black marble, right next to where the N now glowed. Much like its sibling, the blue flame crawled across the stone, but rather than traveling up and down, it moved in a circular motion, leaving the letter O glowing in its wake. The swirling spark, now on the verge of fading out entirely, jumped back onto its perch upon the crimson candlestick. The two blue flames burned menacingly high above the stone, admiring their work. The children stared at the word written onto the black stone in silence, astonished.

"Look," gasped Aurelia. "We're not alone."

The three children watched the word "NO" glow for several long seconds until it faded out, completely vanishing from the black marble stone as if it had never been there.

The children were too entranced with the Shadow Box to look elsewhere, but had anyone turned a watchful eye to the window, they surely would have noticed the silhouette of the large gangly figure with white hair standing outside, peering in and watching them intently as his shoulders shook with silent mirth.

"If we're not alone, who or what is with us?" Zach questioned in a grave tone, looking back and forth between Aurelia and Vidia.

"Don't ask us," Vidia whispered, gesturing frantically. "Ask the Shadow Box!"

"It must be my parents! Right?" Aurelia had been trying to temper herself but was no longer able to contain her excitement.

Vidia's eyes widened with anticipation. "Let's ask and find out."

You must stop at once, Vidia. You know not what you and your silly friends are inviting in.

Vidia rolled her eyes as V's voice grew even more vicious. *There are six others clamoring for you, but you cannot deny that yours and mine are kindred spirits. We've been calling to each other for years. It's in your blood.* Vidia swatted at the air as if to shoo V away. *I've worked far too hard to lose you now, especially to one of them. Grant me control and I will protect you.* V's words echoed inside Vidia's head. The pain in her ankle grew so great she felt she'd been set on fire, and she hissed, unable to control herself. She knew the sound that pierced the silence of the room was not hers.

"I'm always in control, now get out of my head!" Vidia seethed, and the pain in her leg died down.

"Uh, ok? Don't worry, we knew that already," Zach said, looking at Vidia sideways.

"Shadow in the room, are you my mother?" Aurelia asked hopefully.

The shadow flames grew larger, dancing with excitement as they leaned towards Aurelia. "Shadow in the room, are you my mother?" she repeated. This time the blue flame on the right-hand side of the board went first, jumping off its wick and down onto the black marble, burning a letter N onto the stone. It became more and more dim as it inscribed the letter. Right before it went out, it leapt back up onto its post. Its sibling shadow then took its turn. The blue blaze jumped onto the black marble, etching the letter O, then quickly jumping back onto its wick.

"No," Aurelia read aloud, and her heart sank with disappointment as she stared at the blue glow that faded from view within seconds. She was left with a hole in her heart as she stared at the empty black and gray stone.

"Shadow, are you my father?" she asked, her hope rising again.

The flames grew once more and pointed towards Aurelia, who repeated her question. The flickering blue lights darted back and forth, spelling the word NO yet again. Aurelia's disappointment was quickly replaced with a sense of dread. She looked back and forth anxiously between Vidia and Zach.

"Shadow, what is your name?" Zach asked.

The two flames pointed in Zach's direction, dancing delightedly as if mocking the trio. Zach repeated his question, with determination in his voice. The flames once again took turns leaping off their perches, but had much more to say this time. They jumped back and forth from stone to wick after each letter. Once refueled, each flame plunged back down to write another letter. Neither flame touched the stone at the same time, but they clearly were working together. Each moved in tandem and with impressive speed as they went about their work. The children looked on with both terror and wonder. The blue lights looked more like little shooting stars than flames as they twirled back and forth from the stone and their candles. When they were done, the black marble glowed in a sinister scrawl revealing the word *SUMPRIDE*.

"S-U-M-P-R-I-D-E?" Zach asked, spelling out the letters. "What does that mean?"

The temperature in the room dropped further as the words came out of Zach's mouth. The three children stared at each other, confused.

"Shadow of the night, we don't understand," Vidia said. "What are you?"

Nothing but silence followed as the candles' flames now stood oddly motionless, as if frozen in the darkness of the room.

"What are you? Tell us," Vidia again asked in a commanding tone.

The candles once again grew and danced, inscribing letters on the board one by one. Aurelia read the letters quietly as they appeared.

"V-U-L."

This is none of your business, you prideful little brat! V shrieked within the depths of Vidia's mind.

"You're not real. Get out of here!" Vidia snapped to V, this time out loud.

"It's alright, Vidia, we're here with you," Aurelia reassured her friend. She then took a deep breath and drew her attention back to the marble stone. "V-U-L-T. What is it trying to say?"

The flames continued their work, but sped up quickly inscribing the letters U, R, E, and S.

"Vultures," Aurelia read breathlessly, as the blue word glowed on the stone.

"Vultures?" Zack repeated, his icy breath hitting Aurelia's face, and she grimaced from the frosty sting.

"We should stop," Aurelia whispered.

Zack nodded his head in agreement.

You better listen to your friends, V hissed once more from within Vidia.

"No! We still need answers," Vidia countered. "Shadow, what do you mean by vultures?" As the flames leaned toward her, she let out an exasperated breath, her impatience mounting. "Shadow, what do you mean?"

The candle on the left-hand side of the board jumped off its perch and began writing a letter. The burning sensation in Vidia's ankle coursed through her entire body and she felt as if her insides were boiling.

I'm going to make you listen to me, V foamed. Her green eyes flashed a shade of deep red, as if a fire was burning within her and her face became twisted and distorted with rage.

"LEAVE US BE PRIDE, THE CHILD IS MINE!" The words came out of Vidia's mouth in a strange, ancient voice that was clearly not hers. She jerked her head backwards and slammed her fist down on the black marble with such force that the stone cracked down the middle. The small blue flame became trapped within the crack she created before it could finish its first letter, made a loud popping sound for a moment, and fizzled out.

Its sibling then jumped off its wick, and directly toward Vidia's face. Vidia instinctively covered her eyes, shielding herself. The flame landed on the back of her hand, and she felt a deep, aching coldness unlike anything she had ever felt in her life. The second flame faded away as a popping sound yet again filled the room, and on the back of Vidia's right hand the letter "V" glowed in a dull blue print.

"Your hand. There's a V on it!" Zach said, pointing. The glowing blue letter faded away as soon as he spoke, and the coldness in the room lifted.

"You're bleeding," Aurelia exclaimed, grabbing her friend's hand to inspect the deep gash on it from breaking the board.

"I'm fine," Vidia said, snapping back to herself.

"Are you sure?" Aurelia asked with concern. "You should have seen your face when you slammed into the board. Really creepy. No offense. What were you even saying?"

"I don't know. My ankle was just hurting badly. I got bit by a snake the other day, and I think it's getting worse." Feeling defensive after her strange outburst, Vidia lifted her pant leg to reveal her festering wound.

"Whoa. That looks nasty. I can smell it, too," Zach said, baffled by how casually Vidia brought the topic up.

"Oh, my goodness. That looks horrible! It's definitely infected. You need to go to the doctor and get it looked at!" Aurelia said with a look of worry.

"It's fine," Vidia repeated, waving her hand dismissively as she climbed off the bed. "I'll tell my parents tomorrow after Halloween. Don't you two dare say anything. I'm not missing out on Halloween." She glared aggressively at both her friends, hoping they wouldn't rat her out.

Aurelia and Zach exchanged a concerned glance, but before either could say anything, Vidia moved on.

"Well," Vidia continued, "this was just a waste of time. We learned nothing, and now this thingy is broken." She ran her fingers across the large crack on the board.

"Nothing? We learned a lot. We're not alone," Aurelia said quietly.

These words had an impact on all three of them, and the room went silent as they pondered the bizarre events of the night. After a couple of moments, Zach piped up. "Well, this was... different. Hanging out with the two of you is always interesting. I think I've had enough of an adventure for Halloween morning. Time for me to head home before my parents wake up."

"Me, too," Vidia agreed.

"Don't forget the Shadow Box," Aurelia pointed back to the bed.

"It's busted. I don't want it anymore. You can have it. Or throw it away," Vidia responded.

"It's just a crack. I'm sure it can be fixed. I'll keep it," Aurelia said eagerly, still very much hoping it might somehow help her reach her parents.

The children said their goodbyes, and Zach and Vidia headed down the street toward their homes. After a couple of minutes, Zach stopped and turned toward the woods.

"What is it?" Vidia asked, trying not to sound scared.

"There's someone else here," Zach murmured, barely audible.

Vidia reached into her backpack and pulled out a flashlight and shined it in the direction of the woods. The hair stood up on Vidia's neck as her flashlight caught the reflection of several sets of glowing eyes staring back at them.

"It's just animals, right?" Vidia asked as her eyes locked with a set of blazing red beady eyes that appeared to be just at the edge of the woods, much closer than the others.

"Hope so. C'mon, let's hurry," Zach said. They walked briskly in silence the rest of the way home, and although neither one would have admitted it, they were both happy to have the other's company.

"Well, this is me," Zach said, stopping at the bottom of his driveway. "Did you want me to walk with you the rest of the way to your house?"

"I'm fine. It's only a little farther," Vidia responded.

She continued walking again, but within a few seconds paused and hesitated. She looked back at Zach and decided to swallow her pride. "Can you just wait outside until I get to my house?"

"For sure," Zach responded.

"Thanks." Vidia was genuinely grateful of Zach for once.

Vidia walked as briskly as she could without running. When she arrived at her front door, she waved to Zach who was sitting on his front porch.

Once inside her house, she felt a huge sense

of relief and locked the door behind her with a heavy, thankful sigh. As she climbed the stairs to her bedroom, the pain in her ankle returned. With each step the throbbing grew worse and worse, and Vidia felt her fury building with the burning sensation. *Why haven't Mom and Dad noticed my ankle? Something is clearly wrong with it.*

You know why, it's Della's fault. They don't care about or notice anything else anymore, V whispered. *Not even your horrible, festering infection.*

As Vidia passed by her sister's bedroom, she opened the door to the nursery and slithered in. She stood over Della's crib, narrowing her eyes and glaring hatefully at her cherubic sister as she slept peacefully. "This is all your fault," she spewed in a demented whisper, then reached down and squeezed her cheeks aggressively. Della's face contorted into a grimace, and Vidia realized she'd better leave before Della woke and her parents came in. She hastily sped out of the room, but not before swiftly unswaddling Della, leaving her blanket a wrinkled mess underneath the tiny newborn.

Vidia climbed into her bed, looking forward to finally going back to sleep. As she situated herself under the covers, she heard Della begin to cry. Her parents' bedroom door creaked open, and her mother let out a weary sigh as she walked down the hall and into Della's nursery.

Pleased with herself for upsetting her baby sister and making more work for her exhausted mother, Vidia smiled and drifted off into a peaceful slumber.

CHAPTER 11:

THE WITCHING HOUR

Vidia had been working enthusiastically on the final touches of her Halloween costume for nearly an hour. She was determined to look like a *real* witch, not just a girl dressed up as a witch. She pressed carefully into her new wart that sat at the tip of her nose and cackled menacingly into the mirror. Vidia was very pleased with herself for having created such a realistic wart with nothing but maple syrup, peanut butter, and a squishy, old raisin.

Now she just needed to cover it up with something more flesh colored. She reached into her pocket and pulled out her mom's face powder. Charlotte would not be happy if she knew Vidia had gone through her makeup, but Vidia decided this was a night it was worth getting into a little trouble. It was Halloween, after all. Vidia smeared the beige powder carefully onto the raisin and was delighted to see how well it blended with her natural skin tone. She stared at herself in the mirror for a moment, admiring what she saw.

Hmm. Something is still missing, she thought. *Aha! Got it.* Vidia grabbed a pair of scissors out of the medicine cabinet and snipped a scraggly stray hair off the top of her head. She snipped at it until it was about half the length of her pinky finger, dipped the tip of it into the maple syrup, and gently placed the sticky end on her new wart. She clapped with approval at herself. "Every respectable witch has at least one nasty wart," she said gleefully and danced with delight as she cackled once more.

Vidia's excitement was now impossible to contain. Halloween was finally here, her costume was impeccable, and trick-or-treating was hours away. She inspected herself yet again from head to toe, this time smiling and posing. She wore the witch's hat from the attic and a flowing, gothic-style black dress. The dress was a bit too long, so Vidia had taken scissors to it herself, purposefully shredding and fraying the edges of the sleeves and hem to create a more eerie appearance. The dress was peppered with purple shimmering stones that sparkled in the light, and she sported a wide, black belt with a large, silver buckle. Her boots, she decided, were her favorite part of the outfit. She kicked her foot out to stare at them yet again. The sleek, Victorian shoes had perfect pointy toes, laces running up the length of the boot to her calves, and silver buckles near the bottom that perfectly matched her dress. She'd spent days searching for the perfect pair of witch's shoes. She wasn't looking for any old costume shoes. When she finally saw this pair, she knew nothing else would compare. They were stunning, made entirely of leather, and just what she was looking for. Her parents had recoiled at the price.

"Who would spend that much money on something you wear once?" her dad had questioned.

Vidia bristled at his reaction. "It's a special day. What about Mom's wedding dress?"

Dad had laughed uproariously at this comment, causing Vidia to fume in anger. Never one to give up when she set her mind to something, Vidia hassled her parents for weeks before they finally agreed they would pay for half if she paid for the rest. In her left hand she held a kitchen broom she had spraypainted black. She had teased her hair until it was enormously frizzy, and flowed freely and wildly around her face.

Ready for the night, Vidia walked downstairs with a flourish, waiting on the rest of her family in the foyer. Her neighborhood hosted an annual pizza party at the park every year before trick-or-treating began, and Vidia was impatient to head out. "Isn't Della up yet?!" Vidia bellowed up the stairs, annoyed and hoping to wake her sleeping sister.

Dad walked over to the top of the staircase, looked down at Vidia and whispered to her. "I'm sure she'll be up any minute. No need to rush, the party is a couple hours long. We have plenty of time. Now keep it down. Della was up almost all night, and when she finally fell asleep, she woke up screaming hysterically an hour later. Now she's catching up on her sleep, and we don't want her to be cranky and overtired on Halloween."

Vidia stomped her foot as she watched her dad disappear back down the hallway. Vidia spewed hatefully under her breath. "It's ridiculous we're all waiting on that brat. And they say I'm the spoiled one? We all have to wait until she wakes up? She's making all of us late!" She purposefully stomped back and forth across the foyer, her boots loudly clacking across the wood flooring. "Up all night? What a joke. Babies can sleep whenever they want. I won't stand for this any longer."

Atta girl, wake that snot-nosed slug up, V giggled into Vidia's ear.

Vidia mumbled under her breath in response to V. "Stop pestering me right now. I already know Della is ruining everything." She looked out the foyer window and saw Aurelia in the distance, walking with her grandmother. *Great, Aurelia's never beat me to the Halloween party before. We're definitely going to be the last ones there at this rate. I knew this baby would ruin Halloween before she was even born!*

Her ankle started to itch and she bent down

to unbuckle her boot and inspect it. Her skin had turned purple and black around the wound. As she scratched at the raised bite, yellow pus began to seep out. A foul smell permeated the room, and for the first time Vidia was worried she had waited too long to tell her parents.

Should I just tell Mom and Dad about this right now? she pondered.

We can't, look at it. It's starting to turn black. They'll take you to the hospital, and we'll miss trick-or-treating. Tell them tomorrow.

Nodding her head in agreement, Vidia replied to V. *I can't believe they haven't noticed it.*

Of course they haven't. They have barely even looked at you since Della came home. She's taken everything over.

You're right. And now we're going to miss the Halloween party.

Wake her up, V demanded. *You did it so well early this morning.*

I can't right now without Mom or Dad seeing me, Vidia retorted.

A smile then crept across Vidia's face as she formed a plan. She stomped loudly upstairs into her bedroom, climbed onto her bed without removing her boots, and began jumping as boisterously as she could. After a couple of minutes, she realized it wasn't working. She then jumped off her bed hitting the floor with a thud. Still her sister slept. She opened her door, dejected and ready to give up.

Slam it as hard as you can, V whispered in an oddly sweet tone.

But that will be too obvious. Then I'll be in trouble for sure.

If you don't want to miss the party, slam the door.

Vidia didn't need much convincing and slammed her door as loudly as she could. The noise reverberated throughout the entire house.

Mom popped her head out of her bedroom. "What was that?!" she asked in a worried voice.

"Sorry, Mom, I think the wind took it." Vidia sheepishly grinned and pointed to the open window.

"Frank, please shut that window. That was loud, and you know how light of a sleeper Della is." Mom shook her head as she spoke. "I can't believe that didn't wake her." She turned back into her room and shut the door behind her.

Vidia's heart sank as she worried nothing was going to wake her sister. She then began to hear a soft whimpering noise coming from across the hall. It quickly turned into an unmistakable cry, much to Vidia's relief.

Mom reappeared immediately. "Alright, let's get Della changed and then we can head out."

It's so annoying how she only moves fast for Della, Vidia fumed to herself. *At least now we can leave,* she reasoned.

"You look great," Dad said as he walked down the stairs. "Mom will be down in a couple of minutes with Della. Let's go wait outside. Come on, I'll push you on the swing for old time's sake." He turned his head to the side and put on a Transylvanian accent as he said, "It vill be a creepy good time." He held out his hands in claw form in front of his face and stuck out his tongue.

As annoyed as Vidia was with her parents, she couldn't help but laugh at her father's ridiculous expression.

"Very good, then. After you, madam." He opened the front door theatrically, ushering Vidia outside. As they got to the rope swing, Vidia hopped on and began swaying back and forth.

For a fleeting moment, V seemed to disappear, and Vidia forgot about Della. She felt a twinge of pity for everything she had put her family through and a sudden level-headedness returned to her. "Your costume looks good, Dad. And your accent gets better every year."

Dad smiled at Vidia, pleased that his daughter finally seemed to be enjoying herself.

"I've had a lot of practice. You were a little vampire three years in a row when you were younger, remember?"

"Yeah, Dad. I remember you dressing up with me every time. You've always made Halloween so much fun."

"I hope this year is just as much fun," Dad said, with a hint of sadness in his voice. "Can I give you a push?"

"Dad," she started in a whining tone, "I'm too old for that."

"You're never too old to have a little fun. But I do understand you're not a little kid anymore." He hesitated for a moment and continued. "Vidia, I know our family has become bigger and things are changing. I know you love our family traditions, and that change has always been hard for you. But it's not a bad thing. It might not always be easy especially at the beginning, but I promise you, the addition of your little sister is a blessing. I understand it might not feel like that to you right now, but it will with time. You'll see."

Vidia didn't say a word and turned her gaze away from her father to hide the hurt in her eyes. No matter what anyone said, she worried she'd get half the attention she once did. *Is that really so bad though?* she thought to herself. Suddenly she felt embarrassed at her extreme jealousy and wondered why it consumed her so intensely.

Almost as if he could read Vidia's mind, Frank spoke softly and gently. "Vidia, your mother and I love you so much, and I'm really looking forward to trick-or-treating. When we get home, let's read more Frankenstein together. How does that sound?"

"I'd like to read, but Aurelia's coming over and spending the night, remember?"

"How about just one chapter? I'm sure Aurelia would like it."

"Alright, maybe. Just one chapter, though," Vidia concluded.

Mom finally came out the front door holding Della. Vidia jumped off the swing, excited to be leaving, and started up the street.

"Just one minute," Mom hollered after her as she placed Della in her stroller. "I want to check your snake bite before we head on out."

The sight of Della combined with her mother's comment sent Vidia back into her old, irritable state of mind, and V began hissing.

Your Mom is doing this on purpose. She wants you to miss Halloween, V snarled.

"Mom, it's completely fine. Can we go already?" Vidia responded.

"Not until you let me give it a look."

"Why do you treat me like a little baby? I'm eleven, and I told you it's fine. You saw it yourself the other day and said it looked like it was getting better. Now you're going to make me take off my boot and waste more time? I'm fine! I'll show you tomorrow."

Charlotte thought for a moment. "Okay, you're sure it's healing?"

"One hundred percent sure. The scabs will fall off any day now," Vidia responded.

"Alright, then. Let's go," Mom said, and started pushing the stroller.

Vidia took notice of her family's costumes as they began their walk toward the park. Although she found it annoying when Mom and Dad kept referring to themselves as Mr. and Mrs. Dracula throughout the day, now that they were both in costume, she had to admit they both looked pretty good. The only problem was the bulky stroller, which Mr. and Mrs. Dracula took turns pushing with a chubby pumpkin inside. *What kind of vampires would push around a pumpkin?* Vidia wondered, glaring at Della.

Mom and Dad both gushed over how adorable Della looked in her costume, but Vidia begged to differ. She thought Della looked ridiculous. Still, there was one benefit to having a baby that everyone else thought was cute: she looked forward to their family getting more candy, which luckily Della couldn't eat yet.

As they approached the park, Vidia ran ahead. She opened one of the pizza boxes that was sitting on the table, but much to her chagrin all that remained was greasy residue on the bottom of the cardboard. She pushed it to the side, opening box after box until she reached the last one. Not a single slice of pizza remained. Vidia felt her heart drop, but attempted to push her sadness away.

Vidia spotted Aurelia sitting at a picnic table with Zach and a big group of the popular neighborhood kids. Aurelia smiled and motioned for Vidia to join them, but Vidia crossed her arms and shook her head. She instead took a seat at an empty picnic table and stared angrily, her arms still crossed.

Aurelia walked over and sat down beside her, with her plate and drink in hand. "Vidia, what's wrong?" she asked gently. "I've been waiting for you! I'm so excited for tonight."

Vidia stared back, her face devoid of emotion. "The pizza is all gone," she replied.

"Oh, I saved you a piece." Aurelia picked up a piece of pizza that was on her plate and offered it to Vidia.

Vidia shoved Aurelia's hand away and the pizza flopped to the ground. "I don't want your gross leftovers!" she spewed at her friend, with tears welling up in her troubled eyes.

"They weren't leftovers... I was saving it for you." Aurelia responded quietly, unnerved and baffled by Vidia's outburst.

"Sure you were. I bet you're just saying that now because you feel sorry for me."

"That piece of pizza was earmarked for you," Zach said, joining them. "I asked Aurelia for it three times, and she kept telling me it was for you."

"Well, sorry then. Thanks for thinking of me, but I don't want it," Vidia responded, still sulking, but now a little embarrassed. "Have they said when they're taking the group picture?" she asked, trying to change the subject.

"They just took it. Sorry, you missed that, too," said Aurelia.

Vidia shook her head in frustration. Her bulletin board that hung on her bedroom wall boasted the group pictures from every Halloween since she was four years old. She wouldn't have missed one of these parties for the world.

"Missed it? Can we take another?" Vidia pleaded.

"I'll take another," Aurelia said.

"I know you want another picture of me," Zach teased, "but people are starting to leave." Zach gestured toward the popular kids who were now walking away from the park.

"What are you doing with them, Zach? Come on already, we gotta go," Zach's buddy Ted yelled from the sidewalk.

Vidia glared hatefully at Ted. *How is this tomato-faced jerk one of the popular kids? He looks like a stupid, bumbling toddler in an adult-sized body.* Vidia especially couldn't stand Ted after he'd picked on her for months on end in Sunday school.

"I think that's my cue. Maybe I'll see you two out and about tonight if you're not too chicken." Zack smiled and ran off.

"Wow, some friend Zach is. Why would you ever hang out with anyone who associates with Ted? He's such a jerk," Vidia said as she scuffed at the ground below her, not caring about her prized boots anymore.

Aurelia paused thoughtfully before responding. "Zach has never been to Sunday school with us, maybe he doesn't know."

Vidia scoffed at her friend and rolled her eyes as Mom, Dad, and Della finally arrived at the picnic table.

"Della made us miss everything with the party. It's over now!" Vidia tried her hardest to sound angry but gave herself away when her voice cracked in sadness.

"I'm sorry, hon. I guess we misjudged the timing a bit," Dad replied, putting his hand on Vidia's shoulder. "At least it means you're that much closer to trick-or-treating!"

"We?! No, *you* misjudged the timing! I told you we'd miss it!" Vidia snapped, beginning to lose control.

"Vidia, don't talk to your father like that. Do you understand?" Mom said sternly.

"Yes, Mom." Vidia surprised herself at how quickly she gained her composure. Despite the disappointing turn of events, she still didn't want to miss out on the rest of Halloween.

"Alright. I guess we might as well head home and get set for trick-or-treating," Dad said cheerfully, trying his hardest to change the subject. "Aurelia, you can come too," he added, hoping his daughter's friend would help lighten the mood.

Once back home, Vidia and Aurelia grabbed their pillowcases and were ready to go. They impatiently hovered over Dad as he lit the pumpkins and Mom as she filled a bowl with candy and placed it on the front porch.

"We're ready! Let's hit the road," Dad exclaimed.

"Just one more minute, I need to change Della," Mom said, inspecting Della's diaper.

"I think she's doing this on purpose," Vidia mumbled under her breath.

"Your mom or Della?" Aurelia questioned, looking at her friend sideways.

"I don't know!" Vidia replied spitefully. "Probably Della. Or maybe both of them."

Aurelia stared at Vidia confusedly, shocked that her friend wasn't joking and disturbed by the venom in her voice. She then turned to Vidia's mother. "Can I help?"

"Sure, honey. It's wonderful to have someone your age who is happy to help." Mom sighed and looked over at her daughter. "Vidia, would you want to learn how to change a diaper?"

Vidia wrinkled her nose, more in disdain than disgust. "No way, gross."

"Vidia, go help your Mom," Dad said sternly.

"No, Frank, it's fine. Very disappointing, Vidia, but sadly not surprising. Not with how you've been behaving lately, anyway." Mom then turned to Aurelia. "Thank you again, honey. I really do appreciate it. Let's do this quickly so we can get you back out here to trick or treat."

Vidia clenched her fists as tightly as she could, trying desperately not to let her face show her abhorrence. *Ellie Ellie Cinderellie. Always soooo helpful. Such a little goody two-shoes. Always making me look bad. I'm sure that diaper change will take twice as long with her trying to learn how to do it. How stupid.* As Mom, Aurelia, and Della disappeared into the house, Dad sensed something was upsetting Vidia and tried to comfort her.

"Don't worry Vidia. They'll be right back and then we can go. Just try and calm down."

Calm?! How can we stay calm? V screamed as Vidia watched the other kids beginning to run down the sidewalks in their Halloween costumes.

Vidia glared at her father. "We're going to miss out on all the candy, just like we missed the party."

"We won't. It's just a diaper change. Stop being silly." Dad sighed.

Much to Vidia's relief, Mom, Aurelia, and Della were back outside within a couple of minutes.

"Can we leave now?" Vidia asked impatiently as Dad buckled Della back into the stroller.

"Yup. We're all set," Dad replied. "Let's start with the Brauns' house. Maybe your friend Zach will want to go trick-or-treating with the two of you. After that, let's all go to Aurelia's house and say hi to Mrs. Santiago. Once we've said our hellos, you two can go run ahead. We'll be somewhere behind you with Della."

"Sure. Fine," said Vidia, frustrated and worried about the amount of time that would be wasted at the two houses.

"Do you think Zach will want to go trick-or-treating with us?" Aurelia asked Vidia.

"No. I'm sure he'll be going with all his friends." Vidia realized she was disappointed at the thought of him not joining them and was surprised with herself.

"We're his friends, too," Aurelia said quizzically. "Maybe he'll want to go with us for a little while, at least."

"Ok, fine. Zach can come with us if he wants, but Ted and those other cool kids aren't welcome."

CHAPTER 12:

A Push and a Fall

Vidia walked ahead of Aurelia in annoyance and rang the Brauns' doorbell.

"Trick or treat!" Vidia and Aurelia spoke in unison as Mrs. Braun opened the door. Zack's mom was a middle-aged, stout woman, with streaked gray hair and a warm kind smile.

"Look at all of you. So cute!" She peered over Vidia's shoulder and clasped her hands in delight. "Oh my goodness, what a beautiful baby! Charlotte, she's adorable. You've got to all come inside for a minute. It's been so long since I've held a baby."

"Definitely." Mom laughed, delighted to show off her little pumpkin.

Vidia cringed, yet again offended with Della stealing the show, and worried about how long this was going to take.

As they walked inside, Zach popped his head up from the basement. "Nice costume, Aurelia. You make a great angel."

Vidia hadn't even noticed Aurelia's costume until now. *Ugh, an angel. It's like she's trying to annoy me.* She rolled her eyes with disapproval.

"And what are you supposed to be? A troll?" Zach smirked, teasing Vidia.

"Are you brain-dead? I'm obviously a witch."

"Nah, looks more like a troll. With an ooey gooey hairy booger on your nose!"

"No, it's clearly a witch's wart. Why are you so dense?"

"Ok, ok, I'm just messing. I like your costume. Looks like a witch for sure," Zach patted at the air apologetically, now feeling a bit sorry for Vidia, who could never seem to take a joke. "Come on downstairs, everyone is here. You guys can meet them."

"We don't have time," Vidia snapped, nearly cutting Zach off as he spoke.

"I'd love to," Aurelia disagreed, and followed Zach downstairs.

Much to her disappointment, Vidia found herself following along as well.

"Hey, everyone. This is Aurelia and this is Vidia," Zach yelled over the Halloween music blasting through his parents' old antique stereo as a record spun on top.

"Hey, I'm Terrence." A short boy raised his goblin mask to reveal a friendly face and smiled at the girls.

A girl in a baggy sweater and jeans gave a quick wave with a lollipop in hand. "I'm Anne." As far as Vidia and Aurelia could tell, she wasn't dressed up for Halloween.

"Zach, are these the two you've been talking about lately?" a pretty girl questioned, turning up her nose at them. She held a bronze staff taller than her and wore a flowing white gown. A glittering, sheer gold shawl was draped over her shoulders, wrapped around her waist and flowed all the way down to the ground. Her heavy makeup made her already large brown eyes look huge. She wore a golden crown with emerald-colored jewels that linked together like a chain and looked on at the group imposingly.

Zach looked embarrassed. "I think I've mentioned them once or twice."

"Mhm. Well, anyway, my name is Lynette," the blonde girl said.

Aurelia immediately recognized Lynette as the girl all the kids in the neighborhood were always clamoring to hang out with, but she herself had never met her. She fumbled for words momentarily and then blurted out, "I love your costume. Are you an angel, too?"

Lynette laughed. "Me? An angel? Hon, no way definitely not. I'm Cleopatra."

"Oh, I should have known that! Well, you look beautiful. It's nice to meet you all." After a moment of silence, Aurelia nudged Vidia who glared back at her friend and then nodded her head in agreement, forcing a smile.

"Yes, very nice to finally meet the both of you, too." Lynette returned a smile to the girls that was just as fake as Vidia's.

"Ted, aren't you going to introduce yourself, too?" Zach pushed on the pudgy boy's shoulder to get him to look up.

"I already know those two. We go to Sunday school together," Ted replied dismissively.

"Oh. Well, that's good," Zach shrugged. "Anyway, it's time for me to get dressed, too."

"Hey, what about me! Aren't you going to introduce me?" a young boy called as he bounded down the basement steps.

"Uh yeah, this is my little brother, Rip."

"Yes, I'm Rip, and I'm in first grade. Did you know I'm the youngest in my family and Zach is my big brother?"

"I can tell. You look a lot like him!" Aurelia said sweetly.

"Yeah. He says I was a mistake because I'm so much younger than everyone else, but Mom says I'm a gift from God."

"Oh my," said Aurelia, unsure of what to say.

Rip continued as if he didn't even need a response. "I always ask Zach if I can go out and play with him, but he says I'm too little to keep up, but that's not true. I'm really fast. And tonight, I get to prove it. Mommy is making him take me trick-or-treating." Rip talked a mile a minute as he stood there in his skeleton costume.

Ted groaned, "Really Zach, you didn't say we'd be babysitting your little brother."

Zach rolled his eyes. "My mom said I have to."

"It's nice to meet you Rip. I'm Aurelia. I didn't know Zach had a little brother."

"He also has two older sisters and three older brothers. It's a lot to keep track of, don't worry. Everyone else is much older, which makes me think Zach must have been a gift from God, too. We're like best friends."

"One of seven, wow. I always wanted to have lots of siblings," Aurelia smiled at Zach as she spoke.

"Yeah, it's *great*," said Zach sarcastically.

Rip tugged on Vidia's dress. "You're very quiet. Who are you?"

"I'm Vidia." She stared at Rip, annoyed.

"I really like your costume." Rip nodded his head in approval and continued, "It's so good. You look like a real-life troll!" Everyone laughed. Even Aurelia couldn't help herself.

"I'm not a troll! What is wrong with everyone?!"

"Oh, I heard my brother saying you looked like a troll upstairs. I thought you looked more like a witch but didn't want to be rude."

Vidia glared at Rip and then turned to Zach and shook her head at him.

"All right, I think we introduced Vidia and Aurelia to enough people for one day." Zach laughed and rubbed his little brother's head, making a mess of his hair. "I'll be right back." He then disappeared into the bathroom.

"I haven't seen you girls at school." Anne's words came out as an accusation.

"That's because I'm homeschooled," Aurelia said politely.

"Homeschooled? What's it like having your mom as your teacher?" Terrence sounded genuinely curious. "I've always wondered what that would be like."

"Not my mom. My grandmother, but I mostly just teach myself." Aurelia shrugged. "It's good, I guess."

"And what about you?" Lynnette asked, pointing at Vidia.

"I'm at Rolling Hills."

"Look at you, private school. La-di-da," Ted piped up.

Before Vidia could think of a good comeback, Zack reentered the room in his skeleton costume. "I'm all set. You guys ready to go?"

"It's about time," Ted said and then laughed as he caught sight of Zach's costume. "Looks like you and your little brother are being twin skeletons this Halloween."

"Yeah, but we're rocking it." Zach was embarrassed, but he hid it well and didn't let it show. He then held his hand up to his little brother.

Rip jumped up and smacked his brother's hand with an enthusiastic high five. "We're bad to the bone!" he agreed. "Get it, Ted?"

"Alright, whatever." Ted stood up from the couch and pulled a creepy wolf mask over his face. Much to Vidia's surprise, she found Ted's costume to be quite scary. He towered over the group and was dressed in all black. The fuzzy strange sweatpants he donned looked akin to a wolf's mangy fur.

"Would you two want to go trick-or-treating with us? We're planning on hitting every house in our neighborhood and the next neighborhood over," Zach asked Vidia and Aurelia hopefully.

"You want to invite them? Not sure they'd be able to keep up," Ted interjected.

"Ha, that's funny coming from you," Vidia responded with a pointed look at him. "Either way, no thanks. We're going with my little sister and parents."

"Mommy and Daddy? Wow, you girls scared of the dark, too?" Ted jeered in a condescending tone. Lynette, Anne, and Terrence all laughed at his joke.

"Mommy says it's okay to be afraid of the dark," Rip interjected, sticking his tongue out at Ted.

Vidia's face turned red with anger and she clenched her jaw. "I'm not afraid of anything. Try me." Her eyes narrowed intimidatingly.

"It's nice to spend time with your family. I wish I could be with my parents," Aurelia said, trying to comfort her friend and distract her from what seemed like the beginning of a fight.

"Family time? Do your parents still read you bedtime stories, too? And check under the bed for monsters?" Ted busted out into laughter again, arched his back, and howled as maniacally as he could.

Rip grabbed Aurelia's leg and cowered as he stared up at the boy.

"It's alright, Rip. He's just being rude." Aurelia patted Rip's back.

"I'll say. A rude, big fat turd." Vidia's words came out flatly, and she looked squarely at Ted.

"What did you just call me?" Ted stepped toward Vidia, staring her down.

"You heard me. A big fat turd. Trying to scare me? Please." Vidia smiled disingenuously and then puffed her cheeks out with air, further insulting Ted.

"Alright, you two, come on. Let's not call names," Zach interjected, stepping between them.

"Gross, I knew you'd take the turd's side." Vidia glared at Zach. "Just when I was beginning to think maybe you were different. Come on Aurelia, let's go." Vidia grabbed Aurelia by the arm and rushed up the stairs.

"Hold on you two," Zach hollered as he chased after them.

Zach caught the girls as they reached the front door and were about to leave. "Sorry about Ted. He's not normally so rude, but he can be like that sometimes."

"Sometimes? More like all the time. You shouldn't have let him talk to us like that. It's ridiculous that Aurelia thinks you are our friend. I was right all along."

"I am your friend, Vidia. Both you and Aurelia. How can you say that? I was hoping maybe you'd get along with my other friends, too," Zach replied in earnest.

"Not sure about the rest of them, but that Ted kid isn't nice," Aurelia said as she crossed her arms.

"He'll come around," Zach said confidently.

"He's a turd, and anyone who hangs out with him is a turd, too," Vidia declared. "A smelly turd who—"

Aurelia cut Vidia off. "Please, Vidia, now you're just being mean."

Vidia continued as if Aurelia had never spoken. "A smelly turd who pretends to be friends with people just to invite them into his basement and then let his real friends make fun of them." Vidia spoke in a cold, disconnected voice and walked out the door.

Zach's eyes fell to the ground as Vidia walked out of the house. Aurelia stared at Zach, feeling bad for everyone and not sure what to say. After a long pause, she spoke in a soft tone. "Zachary, I just want everyone to get along. I know Vidia has been difficult, especially lately, but Ted has been very rude to her before, too. And he was pretty mean in the basement just now. You could have defended us."

Rip popped up from the basement, joining in on the conversation. "You're right, Aurelia, Ted is not nice. He's always telling me to get lost when I want to hang out with my brother." Rip then turned to his brother. "Zach, I like your new friends better. Let's ditch Ted and those others from downstairs."

Zach ignored Rip and gave Aurelia a meaningful half smile and replied quietly. "You're right, Ellie. I should have told Ted to stop. Sorry about all that. Hope you have fun trick-or-treating tonight."

"You too, and I'm sure you'll get extra candy going around with Rip. They always give the most candy to cute little kids." She smiled broadly at Rip and waved goodbye as she walked out of the house.

Aurelia caught up to Vidia on the sidewalk. "That was horrible," Vidia huffed.

"It wasn't that bad. How cute was Zach's little brother?"

"Cute? He's so annoying. Let's get out of here."

Much to Vidia's relief, her parents were already at the bottom of the street waiting for them.

"You two took a while. We thought maybe you'd made some new friends," Dad said cheerfully.

"No. Definitely not. Let's go. I can't stand being here any longer," Vidia seethed.

"Alright, alright," Dad replied, looking at Vidia and then over to Charlotte, not sure why Vidia seemed so angry.

"That took way too long. We need to make the visit with Mrs. Santiago quick," Vidia continued, angrily watching all the kids that were already out trick-or-treating.

The walk to Mrs. Santiago's house went quickly as Vidia rushed everyone along, but much to her disappointment, once they arrived they spent far too long chit-chatting and taking pictures. Vidia remained silent with her arms crossed the entire time. Nobody batted an eye at her sullen behavior. In fact, nobody even seemed to notice.

They don't see you anymore. You've been forgotten. V's whisper echoed inside Vidia's head over and over as the others' conversation dragged on. Just when it seemed like it was about to end, the conversation turned to Vidia's least favorite subject of all, Della. Vidia felt as if she was going to burst with rage, disappointment, frustration, and sadness. Her legs started shaking and she began viciously clenching her teeth. *Will this ever end? How much can they talk about a baby? She can't even do anything except cry and eat and poop. And cry some more. It's horrible. She's horrible. Why don't they realize?*

Vidia sighed loudly with relief when the conversation finally ended. She threw her pillowcase over her shoulder, ready to head off. Then she heard Mrs. Santiago's voice yet again. "I know you all want to go, but can I hold her just for a minute? She's so very precious,"

"Of course!" Mom responded. "Frank, can you get her out of the stroller and hand her to Mrs. Santiago?"

Vidia felt as if she was being tortured and finally snapped. Before Frank could respond, Vidia screamed at the top of her lungs. "WE DON'T HAVE TIME! ENOUGH WITH THAT BRAT!" She sounded completely unhinged. *Push the little troll over,* V sniggered, pleased with the outburst and hoping to drive Vidia past her breaking point. Vidia then jumped between the stroller and Mrs. Santiago, screamed again like a feral animal, and shoved the stroller sideways violently. Mom gasped in shock. Dad lunged forward as quickly as he could, catching the stroller as it was toppling over and stopped it from crashing to the ground just in the nick of time. He then brought the stroller upright again and inspected Della, who was now crying loudly. "Della's fine. Don't worry, Charlotte. Not a scratch on her."

"Thank God," Mom said in tears, rushing over to her baby. Mrs. Santiago and Aurelia looked on in horror, stunned by Vidia. Mom gave Della a kiss on her forehead and then turned to Vidia. "Vidia, you're done for the night and grounded until Christmas. What's wrong with you? How could you be so horrible to anyone? And your baby sister, no less. I'm absolutely disgusted with your behavior. We're going home."

Vidia had never heard her mom so angry ever before in her life. Charlotte stared at Vidia for a moment to make sure Vidia understood how serious she was with her. She then looked at Frank and continued. "Frank, you take Aurelia trick-or-treating or bring her back to Zach's house if they haven't left yet. We'll see you later tonight."

She turned to Aurelia and gave her a weak half smile. "Aurelia, I hope you have a lot of fun. Mrs. Santiago, I'm so sorry for Vidia's behavior. Please forgive us. Vidia, let's go. NOW." Mom pointed towards home.

"Mom. No! I'm sorry. Please, please let me go trick-or-treating. It's my favorite night of the year. I'm sorry. Please, don't take this from me." Vidia shook as she spoke.

"You took it from yourself. Say goodbye to everyone. You're going home."

"No. No. No. No." Vidia's voice cracked as she repeated herself.

"You heard your mother. Straight home and to your room. And no sleepover tonight, either. We're very disappointed in you, Vidia," her father said, putting a hand on Charlotte's shoulder.

Realizing she wasn't going to change her parents' minds, Vidia started crying hysterically. "I just knew you two would make Halloween all about Della and leave me out. Everything is so different now."

She looked from person to person. Her mom was now clearly boiling over in a quiet fury, while her dad looked disappointed and sad. Mrs. Santiago's eyes were filled with dread and she seemed to be deep in thought. As Vidia glanced towards Aurelia, she realized her friend looked terrified, even more so than this morning when they played with the Shadow Box. The only difference was that the fear in her friend's eyes was clearly directed at her. Aurelia was afraid of her.

How could this be? she wondered to herself. *We're best friends.* She suddenly realized that her slip-up had not just ruined her night, but everyone else's as well. Unable to bear the weight of the judgment she felt from everyone, she ran home sobbing.

CHAPTER 13:

V IN THE FLESH

Vidia slammed the door to her room and screamed. She wielded her broomstick like a baseball bat and whacked at the pillow on her bed, over and over until she saw feathers fluttering into the air. She then threw the broomstick on the ground and flung off her hat. Vidia had never felt a rage like this one, never in her entire life. She continued her rampage and tore down the Halloween pictures she'd been collecting for years. She ripped at her window curtains until the rods came loose and went crashing down to the ground. She stomped her feet, her eyes full of tears.

Finally, Vidia screamed and kicked a hole in the wall, causing the snake bite on her ankle to burst open as a sharp pain shot up her leg. A combination of blood and pus dripped down her foot and pooled on the floor below her. The pain quelled Vidia's madness for a moment and brought an end to her tantrum. It was a good thing, too, Vidia thought, as she heard her mom enter the house.

"Vidia?!" Mom said sternly, knocking on her bedroom door. "What was all that commotion?"

Vidia remained still, staring at the bedroom door with her eyes narrowed, and didn't respond.

"Vidia, we love you, but your behavior is completely unacceptable. It's time for you to start being a good big sister. There's going to be a lot of changes starting tomorrow. Do you understand?"

Vidia still didn't answer.

"Do you understand?" Mom asked once more, raising her voice.

Realizing a response was the best way to get her mother to leave, she finally responded. "Yup."

"Yup, what?" her mother asked through the closed bedroom door.

"Yup, I'm not a baby. I understand." Vidia responded in a rude tone, with a mocking face, taking advantage of the fact that her mother couldn't see her.

"Alright then. Goodnight," Charlotte responded and started to walk away. She paused and then added "I love you," hoping for a response from Vidia. None came and she walked back downstairs to tend to Della.

The pain from Vidia's ankle reached its absolute worst, causing her to break into a cold sweat. She crawled into bed, leaving behind a trail of infected blood. Her vision started to blur, and she began to wonder whether she was awake or asleep. Her thoughts seemed to become less and less coherent as she noticed a strong, minty metallic taste in the back of her throat. The black and red around the ankle had grown and traveled all the way up her calf. She tucked her legs in, pulled her baby blanket over her shoulders and wrapped her hands around her legs, below her knees. She wept softly to herself and started rocking back and forth.

The bright light of the full moon cast a glow onto Vidia's now bare window and caught her narrowed eyes in its eerie luminescence. They looked reptilian as they blazed in an unnatural green, glowing rage. Vidia's crazed reflection in the window stared back at her and then smiled broadly. It flicked its tongue repeatedly and hissed loudly, unleashing pure hatred and venom.

Est tempus, Vidia. It's time.

Vidia buried her head in terror as the demented reflection bored its eyes into her.

Est Tempus. Do you hear me? V demanded.

Vidia suddenly felt great shame at being reproved with the exact same phrase her parents used when they were upset with her. Vidia lifted her head and stared once more at her reflection as her whole body twisted up internally in horror. Her reflection's snakelike eyes morphed into red, wrinkled, beady orifices. Vidia continued to observe her reflection, terrified, trying to figure out where she knew these eyes from. She then recalled the vulture that had visited her last night.

Let thy despair become mine, my rotting contagion. Dost thou agree? Say yes, and I'll take away all thy pain.

Vidia watched as her reflection nodded in the mirror, unsure if she was truly moving her head or not.

V clapped with glee at Vidia's response, her red eyes blazing wildly as V whispered vehemently. "Thine has become mine."

Vidia's face no longer looked like her own in the blazing glow of the full moon. The youthful innocence of a child was gone. Her cold, empty stare now held thousands of years of despair underneath her furrowed, wrinkled brow. She sat for a moment staring at herself as if in a trance, and slowly her fear melted away. She then straightened her back as if she had an audience, cackled wildly, and began to sing.

It's the creepiest time of year.
Full of nasty fun and fear!
This evil witch is ready to play,
and if you say no, I'll end your day!
In the darkest dark of the night,
this wicked witch is high in flight.
Run in terror, run in fright,
there's no escaping me tonight!
I'll start with your toes
and end with your nose.

What a delicious meaty meal,
Even better than newborn veal!

Her reflection clapped once more and began singing a song of its own. Vidia recognized it immediately as the lullaby her mother used to sing to her.

Sleep little baby, sleep baby please,
The goblin is coming and will make such a mess.
Sleep little baby, sleep baby please,
The goblin is coming to feast on thy flesh.
Sleep little baby, sleep baby please,
The goblin is coming to take you from me.

Seconds became minutes, and minutes became hours. Dad had returned home, the trick-or-treaters had long since stopped knocking, and everyone had gone to bed. Vidia finally drifted off to sleep unintentionally. She was awoken by the pulsating, horrible pain in her leg, uncertain of the passage of time, but feeling more like herself. As she thrashed around her bed in pain, her right arm developed a small, consistent twitch. She smacked her lips and swallowed repeatedly, attempting to rid herself of the odd metallic taste that lingered. A flood of drool spilled from both corners of her mouth.

I hope you got your beauty sleep. It's time, dear, V whispered.

Vidia shook her head, knowing exactly what V was talking about. *I'm not sure.*

EST TEMPUS! V hissed, ripping Vidia's covers off and flinging them against the window. Vidia jumped out of bed and stared at her blanket which now enveloped her window in a manner that seemed to defy gravity. She wiped the sleep from her eyes and began to shiver as an icy coldness overtook the room. Vidia was filled with more dread and fear than she had ever felt in her life. She continued to stare at her baby blanket, watching it quiver against the window as if it were attempting to cry out for help. After a couple of moments, the blanket fell to the floor, revealing Vidia's distorted reflection in the window once more. It smirked at Vidia and pointed towards the door.

EST TEMPUS! EST TEMPUS! V seethed.

Vidia felt as if she was being pushed out of the room with a hard, bony hand on her back. She instinctively looked behind herself, unable to accept or understand that nobody was there. As she looked back, she noticed her witch's hat lying on the ground. She inexplicably felt a strong urge to pick it up and place it back on her head. She did so, feeling comforted in the knowledge that this small, silly action was entirely her own.

She slowly opened her bedroom door and crept quietly out into the hallway and down to her parents' bedroom, listening intently. All she heard was the faint buzz of Mom's bedside fan, and after several minutes she was confident they were both asleep. She smiled and blew them both kisses through the closed door.

"I love you, Mommy, I love you, Daddy. See you in the morning."

She tiptoed back down the hall, stopping at the nursery door. She turned the door's handle and as she started to open it, the top hinge let out a loud, pained squeal. Vidia paused and clenched her teeth, hoping it hadn't woken anyone. She stood as still as a statue in the doorway for what felt like an eternity.

Once she was certain Della's slumber hadn't been disturbed, she took off her witch's hat, turned her body sideways and slipped into the room through the cracked door. She gingerly placed her hat back on, and closed the door as slowly as she could. She slinked over to the crib and stood over her baby sister, eyes still blazing, as her brows furrowed and her wrinkles deepened. Vidia watched Della's tiny chest rise and fall with each breath as she slept. Vidia felt a sensation she couldn't quite place tugging on her heart. She was not sure whether it was affection, guilt, or perhaps even love, but she was suddenly overwhelmed. Vidia gripped the crib rail tightly and shook her head. "This is wrong, V."

Such a feeble, weak child you are, V spewed venomously. *It's no wonder your parents prefer that delectable little baby. EST TEMPUS. EST TEMPUS. Now is the time!*

Vidia could not form words and began backing away from the crib in protest. Her ankle again began to throb, but within seconds, the pain was gone, and her entire body was overtaken by a strange numbness.

"You forget, child, you already invited me in."

It then dawned on Vidia that she was hearing V's voice reverberating through the room rather than inside her head. It was much deeper than expected and had a thick, ancient-sounding accent that she couldn't place. She followed the direction of the voice to the mirror that hung on the opposite side of the room. What she saw looking back was surely not her. The reflection's red beady eyes burned into Vidia's. A nasty crooked smile crept across its face as Vidia stared. It reached a pale, blueish-white gaunt arm out of the mirror, followed slowly by the other. Vidia recoiled in horror, noticing strange cracks in V's arms and hands which gave its skin a serpent-like appearance. Its long, skinny hands were that of a human, but in place of fingernails, white talons curled around the bottom corners of the mirror, gripping it tightly.

V braced her talons on either side of the looking glass and pulled herself out of the mirror, as if she was emerging from a swamp, and then fell to the floor. Her chest began to rise and fall heavily. She gasped deeply for air through her twisted smile, and the scales on her cheeks began to crack and peel as if she hadn't taken a breath in a thousand years. The sound of her heavy breathing seemed to shake the entire room. She stared up at Vidia from the floor and her wrinkly eyes narrowed. She slithered across the ground as if she didn't have arms or legs, and stopped at Vidia's feet. She pulled herself upright, struggling to find her footing, until she was face to face with Vidia.

V was dressed in a Victorian nightgown, yellowed with time and completely filthy. It was covered in ruffles and flowed down to the top of her ankles. She leaned her head against Vidia's to steady herself, and her icy cold breath smothered Vidia's face as she spoke. "Free. Finally, free. Let us finish this together."

Vidia shook her head. "How can you be here? You're not real." She looked back at the mirror and was stunned to see no reflection at all.

V giggled. "I'm as real as you are, silly girl. You say no to me as if you have a choice."

"You're nothing more than my mind, my jealousy."

"Oh, but that's where you're wrong, child. You invited me in with your envy, that much is true. Never have I had a keeper with such spite, such malice, and all over the pure innocence of a newborn baby. How powerful a team we will now make. EST TEMPUS." V cackled and reached out her spiny hand.

Too weak and tired to resist any longer, Vidia gave in to the inexplicable darkness that overwhelmed her. Taking V's hand, she felt a twisted sense of welcoming.

Dad sat up in bed, confused by the sound of the phone ringing so late at night. Wondering who could possibly be calling at this hour, he answered the phone groggily. "Hello?"

"Frank, check the bebé," a frantic voice whispered through the receiver.

Inside the nursery, Vidia and V turned towards the crib, hand in hand. Vidia slipped into a complete state of delirium and began chanting along with V. "Est tempus. Est tempus."

"What? Who is this?" Dad responded, still waking up.
"Check the bebé, Frank. Check her right now."

Vidia and V stood over Della's crib, staring down at the baby. Vidia smiled maniacally and started to softly sing. "I'll start with your toes, and end with your nose."

"Go on, then," V insisted. Vidia reached down to grab her sister, but then realized she would probably wake her up. Thinking quickly, she climbed into the crib with her. She took her sister's blanket off and tucked a corner of it underneath her collar. "We don't want to make a mess," she giggled as she positioned her makeshift bib.

"Mrs. Santiago, is that you?" Dad questioned, now more alert as he began to recognize the voice on the other end of the phone.

"Frank, go check baby Della right now! Before it's too late!" Mrs. Santiago now yelled in desperation.

Vidia raised Della's little foot to her mouth and looked down. Della opened her eyes and smiled up at her sister, cooing at the familiar face. Even amid her wild delirium, Vidia could see the innocent baby looking up at her with love.

"What's wrong with me?" Vidia questioned, suddenly disgusted with herself. "I won't do this."

"WE MUST!" V screamed at the top of her lungs and jumped into the crib.

An abrupt dread overwhelmed Frank as he dropped the receiver while Mrs. Santiago continued to plead into it. He jumped out of bed, and as his feet hit the ground he suddenly heard a demented, unrecognizable scream coming from the nursery. He sprinted down the hall and flung open the nursery door. To his horror he saw Vidia sitting in the crib holding Della's foot in her hand, pressed tightly against her closed mouth as she rocked back and forth.

"Vidia, what are you doing? Get out of there!" he yelled.

Vidia stared blankly in the direction of her father, but did not seem to see or hear him.

"Everything will finally go back to normal now. Est tempus," she said calmly. She closed her eyes and opened her mouth as widely as she could. Frothy drool dripped down her chin and her body quivered in an unnatural manner, in the same way her baby blanket had vibrated against her window.

Dad lunged across the room and yanked Vidia out of the crib, saving Della from any harm as Vidia bit down as viciously as possible. She gnashed her teeth together with a monstrous force that was far greater than that of any human, tearing through her father's flesh and splintering the bone underneath with ease.

"Vidia, stop!" Dad thundered, horrified with his daughter. He gripped Vidia firmly in a bear hug to still her flailing body as blood from his severed finger gushed all over.

Mom then appeared at the doorway, having woken from the commotion. As she observed the scene she began screaming in terror. Vidia looked up at her and smiled, open-mouthed, ear to ear, revealing Dad's severed finger between her teeth.

Her mother's eyes flashed as if she suddenly understood what was happening. "ABSIT VIDIA! Peccatum, be gone!" Charlotte's strange words caused Vidia to thrash violently back and forth in her dad's arms, and then all at once she stopped.

After a couple of moments, Vidia realized she was no longer in the crib but being held tightly by her father, and it wasn't Della's toe she was eating, but her father's index finger. Vidia spit out the bloody finger, and it rolled across the room, stopping at her mother's feet.

"What have I done?!" Vidia cried out, the words tearing from her throat in a strangled sob of despair.

CHAPTER 14:

ROOM 517

Aurelia twisted her hands nervously, unable to focus on the reverend's sermon. It had been nearly a week since Vidia's meltdown on Halloween, and she hadn't heard a word from her friend since then. Aurelia stared ahead at Mrs. Gardner, who was surrounded by empty pews and busy swaying and shushing her newborn. Something had to be wrong, Aurelia thought worriedly. The Gardners always attended church together.

Aurelia tugged on her abuela's arm. "Where do you think Vidia and Mr. Gardner are?" she whispered.

Mrs. Santiago glanced over at Charlotte and Della with a knowing look and sadness in her eyes. "Let us give them space. They will share when the time is right."

Aurelia was not satisfied with that explanation in the least but knew her abuela better than to press any further. She decided she'd figure it out once she got home.

Once church was over and she had walked her abuela home, she hopped on her bike and raced over to Zach's house, anxious and determined to figure out what was going on with her best friend.

"Have you seen Vidia?" she asked abruptly, as soon as Zach opened the door.

"Hello to you, too." He smiled. "And no. Not since she got all mad at me on Halloween. Figured she decided to start avoiding me." Zach walked out and sat on the top stoop of the front porch, motioning for her to join him.

Aurelia remained standing and paced, more anxious than before. "I don't think she'd ever do that. Well, at least I wouldn't. Anyway, I haven't seen Vidia since Halloween either. Something must be up. She wasn't even at church today. Where do you think she could be?"

"I dunno. I wouldn't worry. Maybe she's grounded. Pushing her baby sister's stroller over on Halloween was pretty messed up."

"You didn't tell anyone about that after we went trick-or-treating together, did you? I didn't want to gossip, but I knew you'd ask why I showed up without her and I just had to tell someone what happened!"

"I didn't tell anyone. I bet she's just grounded for doing that. But we can go find out for sure," Zach responded, pulling out several Reese's cups from his pocket. "But first, how about a snack?" he asked.

"No time for candy right now," said Aurelia. "Let's go."

Before Zach could protest, Rip popped his head out the front door. "You better go check on your friend, Zach! I can come too if you want, angel girl?" Rip looked at Aurelia like an eager puppy dog.

"No, we got it. Her name is Ellie by the way," Zach responded before Aurelia could say anything.

"Okay fine, but hand me that candy at least. I'll take care of it for you until you get back," Rip responded with a sly smile.

Zach laughed. "Now I see why you came out here. Don't you still have a ton of candy?" he questioned.

"Nope. It's all gone," Rip replied, hanging his head in faux remorse.

"Alright then, you can take care of mine, and if you really want you can even eat it, too." Zach flipped the pieces of candy, one by one, to his little brother.

"Tell the witch girl I say hi," Rip called out after Zach and Aurelia as they climbed onto their bikes. The moment they turned to head out, Rip stuffed every piece of candy into his mouth at once, looking like a chipmunk as he waved goodbye to his brother and friend.

It was a quick ride, only several houses down the street. Zach played it cool like usual, but they both felt that something was very off about the situation. Once they reached the Gardners' house,

Zach knocked on the front door. When there was no answer, he knocked again as loudly as he could.

After a couple of moments which felt like an eternity to Aurelia and Zach, Mrs. Gardner answered the door, holding Della as she slept in her arms. "Hi, kids," she said in a weary tone, staring blankly ahead.

"Hi, Mrs. Gardner. We were wondering if Vidia wanted to come outside with us," Aurelia said.

"Vidia is not home right now," Mrs. Gardner said flatly.

"Oh, ok." Aurelia paused and decided how best to glean any further information. "I guess we'll come back later then?"

"She won't be home for a long time, Aurelia," Mrs. Gardner's voice shook as she spoke these words, trying to maintain composure.

"Why not? Where did she go?" Zach asked bluntly.

"Is she ok? I've been worried about her," Aurelia added in earnest.

Mrs. Gardner could see the concern on the two children's faces and was overcome with emotion. She was not sure how to broach such a disturbing subject with children but felt they deserved to know. "She tried to hurt her baby sister on Halloween after everyone had gone to bed, but everyone will be alright."

All the color left Aurelia's face, and she began sputtering. "What? I can't believe that. I just... Did she.... What happened?"

Mrs. Gardner turned to the side to cover her face as tears silently fell. "Vidia had a terribly infected snake bite. Her father believes it made her delirious and caused her to act... well, insane. We're worried sick about her. Frank found her in Della's crib, and she ended up biting her father's finger off because he got in her way."

Both children stared incredulously for several seconds. Finally, Aurelia spoke. "We both saw her snake bite. She didn't want us to tell anyone until after Halloween. I'm so sorry I didn't." Aurelia began to cry. "Is Vidia going to be ok? What about Mr. Gardner and Della?"

Charlotte shook her head. "It's nothing for you to feel responsible for. Vidia is doing well in the hospital. Della is perfectly fine, thanks to Frank." Mrs. Gardner stared down at her baby as tears splashed onto Della's little hat. "And Frank, well, the doctors reattached his finger just in the nick of time."

"So, everyone is alright?" Aurelia looked intently at Mrs. Gardner, feeling relieved but horrified at her friend.

Mrs. Gardner drew a long breath. "Yes. But we need to keep Della safe. Vidia will be staying with her grandparents once she's fully recovered and out of the hospital."

"For how long?" Zach asked.

"We don't really know. As long as it takes for her to get better and for us to feel comfortable bringing her around Della again." Charlotte stared at the wide-eyed, dumbstruck children and felt as if she had just dramatically overshared.

"Now you two can keep that to yourselves, can't you? We are heartbroken over everything, and you know how the neighbors gossip."

"We certainly will," Aurelia assured her. "I want to help however I can."

"Yeah," Zach agreed, "we wouldn't do that. Being in middle school is rough enough."

"Vidia is fortunate to have friends like you." Mrs. Gardner smiled weakly. "Alright, you two. Run along and play."

The moment the door shut, Aurelia turned to Zach. "I knew something was wrong. We need to check on Vidia."

"How? You heard Mrs. Gardner. Vidia's not coming home."

"Right, but that doesn't mean we can't visit her. We've got our bikes. The hospital is only five minutes away in the car."

Zach nodded. "Alright, let's go."

After a couple of wrong turns, Aurelia and Zach finally arrived at the hospital nearly an hour later, exhausted.

"You said that was close," Zach said, wiping the sweat from his brow.

"Sorry, I guess it feels closer in the car. But we're here. Now how are we going to get in? I don't know if they'll let two kids without parents into the hospital. Even if they would, I don't want to risk asking. What is it Vidia always says? Better to ask forgiveness than permission." Aurelia laughed. "I'm beginning to understand what she meant."

"Yup. We can sneak in," Zach replied confidently as he scanned the parking lot.

"What are you looking for?' Aurelia asked, not sure what Zach was up to.

"There's a family over there with a bunch of kids. We'll piggyback on into the hospital with them. Stay close and follow my lead."

"No way, we'll definitely get caught," Aurelia protested.

"Trust me, it will work." Zach nodded confidently and darted into the hospital right behind the family of seven. Aurelia followed behind timidly.

"What a cute little guy. How old is he?" Zach said loudly, stepping in front of the large family and cutting off the mom pushing a double stroller.

"Uh, six months," the mother replied, annoyed and already distracted by her wailing toddler who had just run off again. "Lily, get your brother for me! I knew I should have put him in the stroller with Johnny here." She pushed past Zach and quickly walked through the reception area of the hospital.

Zach looked back at Aurelia and motioned for her to follow him. "Let's go. This is our chance." The two of them slipped into the hospital as if they were part of the large family caravan.

"Ok, that was impressive. How were you so sure we wouldn't be noticed?" Aurelia asked. Zach laughed. "When you come from a big family, it's easy to blend in."

"I see. Well, now what? I mean how are we going to find Vidia?" she continued.

"That part is easy. We can ask someone."

"Huh? But what if we get caught?"

Zach shook his head confidently. "Ellie Ellie Cinderellie. I always find my way. Trust me, we'll be fine."

Aurelia awkwardly followed behind Zach. He walked around nonchalantly until he saw a nurse in scrubs covered in silly cartoon images of dogs and cats. He turned back to Aurelia. "There's our mark." He noticed Aurelia's nervous expression and slouched shoulders. "You just gotta be cool. Acting scared is what will give us away."

"Confidence. Got it. Ok, let's do this." Aurelia nodded her head.

Zach walked up to the nurse who was busy staring at a clipboard. "Excuse me, we just went down to the cafeteria for some food and can't find our way back to our cousin's room anymore. Could you help us find her?"

"No problem, honey," the nurse replied cheerfully. "What's her last name?"

"Gardner."

The nurse's eyes widened a little as she searched the roster. "Vidia?" She shivered as she said the name, knowing exactly why Vidia was at the hospital.

"You got it," Zach said, peering over at the paper.

"How long have you kids been wandering around lost?" The nurse laughed, trying not to show how unsettled she was. "You have a bit of a walk. Follow down this hallway and make a right. It's all the way on the north end of the hospital. You'll see a sign for pediatrics, turn left at the sign. You'll then see a big set of double doors, turn right there and keep going. Once you see the elevator, go up to the 5th floor and take another right when you get off. Follow the signs for recovery. You can just follow that until you get there. Room 517."

Aurelia stared like a deer in headlights at the complicated directions and Zach quickly piped up.

"Thanks so much," he responded.

Aurelia put on a thick English accent and said, "Goodness me, we really did get turned around didn't we. Thank you kindly for the directions, ma'am." She then curtsied ridiculously in front of the nurse.

"You're welcome?" the nurse responded, looking utterly confused as she walked away.

Zack looked at Aurelia sideways and couldn't help but smile. The moment they were out of the nurse's earshot, Zach burst into laughter. "What was that?"

"I was in the moment, selling our story," Aurelia responded seriously.

"Selling our story? Why would cousins have different accents?"

"I don't know! I could be a relative visiting from England."

"I can tell you've never done anything sneaky before. Or if you have, you definitely haven't gotten away with it," Zach joked, still trying not to laugh too loudly. He then paused, hoping he hadn't offended Aurelia and added, "But that was a solid first effort."

After walking for several minutes, they found themselves at room 517. Aurelia peered into the door, which was already halfway open. "We found her," she whispered to Zach.

"Ok, great. Let's go in and check on her."

"Not yet. We can't. Mr. Gardner is sitting right beside her! We'll have to wait until he leaves."

"That could take all night, and what if he doesn't leave at all?" Zach questioned.

Then they both heard a phone ring from within the room. "Hello?" Mr. Gardner said, followed by several seconds of silence before he spoke again. "Yes, yes Mrs. Santiago, everything is ok." Both Aurelia and Zach exchanged glances with each other as they listened intently to his side of the conversation. "Thank God, you called me the other night. How did you know something was wrong?" Mr. Gardner's voice was full of worry. He then nodded his head repeatedly for a couple of moments and continued. "Hold on. I need to step outside. I don't want to disturb Vidia while she sleeps."

Aurelia and Zack darted around the corner to a small waiting area with several chairs just as Mr. Gardner left the room.

"This is our chance. It's now or never," Zach said.

"Let's go," Aurelia agreed.

They quietly crept into the room, and Aurelia walked up to the bed where Vidia slept. She noticed the deathly pallor on her friend's face and felt sick to her stomach. If not for the small rise and fall in her chest every couple of seconds, Aurelia would have thought Vidia was dead.

"Vidia? Can you hear us?" Aurelia questioned, her voice trembling.

"We wanted to check on you and make sure you're ok," Zach added, pacing back and forth at the door, keeping an eye out for Mr. Gardner.

Aurelia took Vidia's hand. "We heard what happened from your mom. I just can't believe it. I know something's not right. I can feel it in my bones. Please don't worry, we're here for you."

The lights in the room began to flicker and make an eerie zapping noise, then went out entirely. An icy chill enveloped the room and Aurelia gasped in horror.

"Not again," Zach groaned, his breath forming frost in the air. He raced over to the window to open the blinds. Although the sun was beginning to set, they were able to see relatively clearly again. Suddenly, they heard a loud pounding outside the window. Aurelia and Zach both froze in fear for a split second, wondering if they had been caught. They then realized an enormous vulture had landed on the small railing outside the hospital window.

It stared directly at Vidia, eyeing her like a meal, and cawed loudly. It locked eyes with Aurelia and backed away to the end of the railing, but remained, staring and carefully watching her.

"Wow. I think it's scared of you, Ellie."

"I was thinking the same thing," Aurelia commented quietly, clasping her mother's cross necklace that hung from her neck. She then turned her attention back to Vidia and placed her hand gently on top of hers. "She's chilled to the bone. And it's definitely getting colder and colder in here. Something is wrong."

As Aurelia went to let go of her hand, Vidia squeezed with a vice grip and Aurelia was unable to break free of her iron grasp. Vidia's eyes remained shut, but her eyeballs moved back and forth wildly beneath her closed eyelids.

"Vidia? Can you hear me?" Aurelia questioned, her heart now pounding in her chest.

All at once, Vidia let go of Aurelia's hand, sat up with a jolt, slowly raised her arm, and pointed at the mirror with her eyes still closed.

"What is she doing?" Zach whispered, forgetting his post at the door and joining Aurelia by Vidia's bedside.

"Look," Aurelia said, motioning towards the mirror.

In the frosty mirror, they could see what appeared to be Vidia, but her skin was cracked, weathered and covered in scales. The reflection's eyes were wide open and glowing in a blazing, fiery red. The creature then began scratching words on the inside of the mirror in the frosty condensation. The noise was deafening and akin to nails on a chalkboard. Its long, skinny, cracked fingers spread across the mirror, revealing white birdlike talons in place of fingernails.

Aurelia read the words out loud as they appeared. *You're too late. Leave now, or I'll eat you too.*

Aurelia squinted as if she couldn't believe her eyes. "Eat... us, too?" she said in a terrified whisper.

The reflection smiled like an insane clown, with its grin contorting unnaturally and running across the entire length of its face. The thing then raised a talon, and pointed it at Aurelia and then Zach. Its enormous, razor-sharp talons were now on full display, clearly meant to intimidate the children. The creature slowly ran its claw across its neck, as if it was slitting its own throat. It ended the motion with a flourish and smirked maliciously.

It then spoke to them with a thick, unidentifiable accent. "You have been warned," the voice boomed, echoing through the room, as the mirror cracked down the middle.

Suddenly the lights came back on, but much brighter than before. They continued to burn brighter and brighter, until every bulb in the room burst with a deafening, shattering noise. Aurelia and Zach shielded their faces as the room went dark again and bits of glass rained down on them from above. Vidia fell back down in her bed, and the reflection was gone.

Both children stood frozen. Finally, Zach broke the silence. "Did that really just happen, or am I seeing things?" His voice shook as he spoke.

"I wish we were both seeing things. But look, the words are still there." Aurelia stared at the cracked mirror as the scratched words in the frost faded out and the temperature of the room returned to normal. "Now I have even more questions than before we got here," Aurelia continued.

Zach paced back toward his lookout post at the door. "Me, too, but there's no time. Mr. Gardner is coming back!"

Tears welled up in Aurelia's eyes. "We can't leave her."

"We'll come back and check on her again. She's fine with her dad," Zach whispered.

Aurelia nodded and then turned back to Vidia. "We'll figure out what's happening. Don't worry." With that, she quickly scurried out of the room and into the busy hallway with Zach.

CHAPTER 15:

THE SHEPHERDS' BURDEN

As Aurelia pushed open the doors to the hospital's exit, she couldn't contain herself any longer. Tears flooded her face as she spoke to Zach. "I can't believe we just left her there."

"We didn't have a choice," said Zach solemnly, then paused a beat and drew a big breath. "That was the scariest thing I've ever seen. Even worse than that night with the Shadow Box."

"Yeah," Aurelia agreed. "Something is very wrong. We have to figure out what's going on and help her. Did you hear who Mr. Gardner was on the phone with?"

"No, but he sounded upset," answered Zach.

"It was my abuela. Mr. Gardner was asking her how she knew what Vidia was going to do to Della. How in the world would she know that? I bet she has answers. Ever since I can remember, she's always seemed to have all the answers."

Both children went silent until Zach finally spoke.

"Even if she does have the answers, how does that help us? Your grandma won't tell us anything. She still hasn't even told you what happened to your parents." Zach immediately felt that he'd put his foot in his mouth as Aurelia became even more visibly upset.

"You're right." Her sadness melted away as she then drew her shoulders back and stared at Zach with determination. "But I'm not going to stand for it anymore. My abuela has been acting stranger than ever since Halloween." Aurelia's face turned red with anger. "She told me at church this morning that we needed to give the Gardners space. After hearing that phone call, it's completely obvious she knows what's going on, and she's clearly not giving them any space." Aurelia put her bike helmet on, looked at Zach and continued, her words laced with defiance. "I'm sick and tired of all her secrets! It's time she starts telling me the truth."

"Yeah, but if we talk to your grandma won't that mean we have to tell her we were in your house and that we came to the hospital? Why not just come back to the hospital tomorrow and see if Vidia's awake and we can talk to her?" Zach said, hoping to change Aurelia's mind.

"We should definitely come back tomorrow to check on her, but if we talk to my grandmother beforehand, we'll come back with more answers. Don't worry about Abuela being upset with us. She's really just a big softy, although she'd ground me if I told her I rode my bike to the hospital without asking her first. Let's only mention what happened on Halloween with the Shadow Box. We can't risk getting grounded right now with Vidia stuck in the hospital. She won't be that upset about you guys coming over to the house without her knowing, and even if she gets a little mad, she'll forget all about that once she hears the story. Come on," Aurelia called over her shoulder as she raced down the street.

"We're totally going to get in trouble," Zach mumbled into the wind, fully aware that Aurelia couldn't hear him anymore.

When they reached Aurelia's house, she walked in boldly, with Zach following trepidatiously behind. Mrs. Santiago was standing in the kitchen with her arms folded and her brow slightly furrowed, as if already waiting for them. She skipped a greeting and any small talk, much to Zach's relief.

"Come along and sit down then," the elderly woman said seriously. "I'll pour you both some lemonade and we can have a talk." She then motioned for them to sit at the kitchen table.

"A talk about what?" Aurelia said, giving her grandmother a side eye.

Her grandmother looked slightly amused. "I don't know. You tell me." Her eyes twinkled as if she was sharing an inside joke with nobody in particular.

Aurelia finally let nearly a lifetime of frustration boil to the surface, and for the first time, she didn't hold anything back while speaking to her grandmother. "Vidia is hurt, and I know you know all about it. So, we have some questions for you. And no more evasive answers, ok?" Aurelia's voice shook, heavy with anger and concern. "We deserve the truth."

"Um, maybe I should go," Zach said awkwardly, feeling the tension in the room.

"No. You're a part of this, too," Aurelia said as she stared intensely at her abuela and continued. "He's staying."

Mrs. Santiago nodded her head calmly. "Sit boy, let me pour you some of my homemade lemonade and you tell me if you like it." Her eyes remained on Aurelia the entire time she spoke. Zach sat down without a word.

"You too, Aurelia darling. Sit. My sweet girl, I have never seen you like this. Tell me what's on your mind." Mrs. Santiago placed two tall glasses of lemonade on the table, one in front of Zach and the other in front of Aurelia.

Aurelia sat down and chugged the glass of lemonade within seconds until it was completely gone. "Thanks," she said as she placed the empty glass down, shoved her chair back, and began pacing back and forth.

"Well, go ahead then." Mrs. Santiago motioned impatiently for Aurelia to continue.

"Ok, well here it goes. Me, Zach, and Vidia snuck into Mom and Dad's old room. Actually no, we didn't sneak in, we went in. Because I should be able to go into my parents' room. Anyway, this happened on Halloween morning. Vidia brought a Shadow Box, and I was hoping maybe we'd get to talk to Mom and Dad, but they weren't there."

"Shadow Boxes are not toys to be played with. You should not mess with such things." Mrs. Santiago then grunted and raised her eyebrows. "So you snuck this boy into my house?" she questioned, finally turning to look at Zach.

"Yes. Zach, Vidia, and myself. They're my friends."

Zach took a sip of the lemonade, trying his hardest to change topics and take the heat off himself. "This is really good Mrs. Santiago, best I've ever had. Thank you so much for making it for me." He feigned a smile nervously.

Mrs. Santiago grumbled and stared at the boy a moment longer before turning back to Aurelia. "Go on, Aurelia, continue your much overdue confession."

"Mom and Dad weren't there when we tried to use the Shadow Box. But someone... or something was."

Mrs. Santiago's eyes narrowed. "What happened?" she asked intently, leaning forward.

"The box spelled 'S-U-M-P-R-I-D-E' and 'vultures.'"

"Vultures I understand, but sumpride? That is not a word. Are you sure that's what it spelled?" Mrs. Santiago questioned.

"Yes, definitely," Zach interjected.

Mrs. Santiago pondered, tapping her index finger against her lips. She then furrowed her brow and repeated the word out loud a couple of times, when suddenly it came to her. "Ah! It was not speaking English. What it was saying was 'Sum Pride.' Sum is Latin for 'I am.' It was telling you who it was. 'I am Pride.'"

"Oh, ok. I still don't know what that means. After it spelled all that out, it was like Vidia lost her mind. She slammed herself down on the board and broke it and yelled some crazy creepy stuff. It didn't even sound like it was coming from her."

"Definitely not Vidia's voice. It sounded like an ancient monster," Zach agreed.

Mrs. Santiago once again looked over at Zach, annoyed. "You explored several rooms in my house that night, didn't you, boy?"

Zach didn't know what to say. "Um, maybe?"

"One of those rooms was mine." She pointed at him. "You stood over my bed and you took the keys from my nightstand. I was not dreaming that night when I saw you staring down at me, was I?"

Zach hesitated for a moment and spoke. "No, you weren't dreaming. I'm so sorry. I should never have gone into your room. I was trying to help Aurelia figure out what happened to her parents. I think she deserves to know." Once again Zach immediately regretted sharing his feelings on the subject.

Mrs. Santiago stared at Zach, intently tapping her finger against her pursed lips. After what felt like an eternity to Zach, she finally fixed her attention back on Aurelia and spoke. "Is that why you now wear your mother's cross around your neck? I've been wondering why you didn't ask me before you took that." Mrs. Santiago paused, then smiled softly. "You are old enough now to claim it as your own. It's a family heirloom, from your mother. My wonderful Annabelle. Before it was Annabelle's it was mine, and before that, it belonged to my mother, and her mother before her. It's been in our family since the beginning. Did you know that?"

Aurelia shook her head and stared down at her necklace. "I didn't. I'll take good care of it, Abuela."

Mrs. Santiago smiled quickly and nodded, then her brow furrowed again as she was brought back to the uncomfortable subject at hand and sighed deeply. "Seeing usually comes so easily to me, but not so much with you, Aurelia. Love has a tendency to cloud the mind."

"I'm not sure what you mean by seeing." Aurelia paused, taking the necklace in her hand and continued. "It's a family heirloom, and you're not mad at me for taking it? Or for going into my parents' room without your permission?"

"Maybe I should be. But no, mija, I'm not upset with you. I know you have an inquisitive heart and mind, just like your mother. You're also getting older. I do understand that you're growing up, so I am happy to see that necklace on you. It's especially good that you're wearing it now."

"Great news!" Zach interjected. "I was sure you'd be so mad at us. Glad we sorted this all out." Zach looked very relieved as he took another swig of lemonade.

Mrs. Santiago glanced back at Zach with a look of surprise, almost as if she had forgotten he was there. "I'm not happy with you, boy," she said curtly as her eyes narrowed yet again.

Zach gulped nervously, coughing a bit as he choked on his drink.

Mrs. Santiago then turned back to Aurelia and asked, "He is your friend, yes?"

"Zach is my best friend," Aurelia responded. "Well, Zach and Vidia."

Mrs. Santiago strummed the table with her fingers for a moment, deliberately tapping each finger with force against the tabletop, staring intently at Zach. She stood, poured them both more lemonade and sat back down pensively. Both children waited with bated breath. Mrs. Santiago then clasped her hands together and bowed her head in prayer. Aurelia and Zach looked at each other in confusion as Mrs. Santiago whispered inaudibly for several long seconds. She closed with an "Amen," raised her head, and looked at the children earnestly.

"Alright, then. I can see that it is now time for you to learn of our family's past, my darling Aurelia."

She paused. "And you too, Mr. Zach. We always must shepherd in groups of three. Aurelia, Vidia, and Zach, the Shepherds of the Lost. Yes, that has a nice ring to it."

"Shepherds of the Lost? What do you mean?" Aurelia asked, perplexed.

"Good question. Where to start? Our family has been tasked with a great responsibility, dating back hundreds of years. We are among the last remaining Shepherds."

"I still don't understand," Aurelia interrupted. "For starters, what is a Shepherd?"

"I will try to explain the best I can. There is another world that exists between this life and the afterlife called the In Between. For all of time, now and forever, there has and will always exist the In Between. Many souls from our world have lost their way, and unknowingly found themselves within the confines of the In Between."

"How does that happen?" Aurelia questioned.

"We don't entirely know. All I can tell for certain is that its chief purpose seems to be to serve as a gateway."

"A gateway to what?" Aurelia asked.

Mrs. Santiago shuddered. "Nothing good, at least not that I've ever seen. I believe our transgressions or possibly weaknesses open the barrier, and at times we unknowingly find ourselves there. We drift in and out. Many of us will never know all the times we've been there. It starts as a state of mind, almost a dream-like state. On its own, I believe it to be neither good nor bad, just an icy cold, uncomfortable place to be. The problem is that many ungodly creatures also reside within the In Between, hungry and waiting in the shadows to prey on their next earthly meal. They hunt those who have lost their way, and find themselves bouncing back and forth between our world and the In Between. Sometimes, these travelers completely lose their way and fall prey to the creatures of the In Between until their actual, physical self decays into the In Between. It is at this point that one's soul becomes imprisoned, trapped there. These poor souls have no sense of self left. We call them the Haunted.

"This, children, is where we Shepherds come into the picture. Our job is to bring lost souls, especially the Haunted, home. We are the Shepherds of the Lost, protectors of the forgotten. We Shepherds voyage into the In Between with an important mission, to guide the haunted souls out of the depths of darkness and back to our world. The task is always ripe with danger for a Shepherd."

"Wicked!" Zach interrupted, sounding fascinated. "So, you were a Shepherd? Or are you still one?"

Mrs. Santiago looked so offended Aurelia piped in to clear up any misunderstanding. "He means wicked, as in cool."

"Ok, boy. To be clear, Shepherds are not wicked. Quite the opposite, and I wouldn't call any of this cool, either."

"I'm beginning to think you are very cool, Mrs. Santiago," Zach said.

"Zach, stop joking around. This is serious. Go on, Abuela, tell us more."

"Sí, Aurelia, we have much to worry about. We are not always successful in shepherding the lost back into our world. In truth, we fail more than we succeed. It is a very difficult job full of heartbreak and disappointments, but we must do everything we can. Our earthly world relies on our successes. Evil will fester and grow if we let it. Always."

Mrs. Santiago paused a moment to let her words sink in before continuing, "The evil creatures in the In Between are constantly watching us, hoping our world will decay into darkness and with it, the barriers between worlds. We Shepherds do everything possible to keep our world safe from theirs. Unfortunately, there are not many Shepherds left. I am still a Shepherd, and your uncle Elvis is as well. Your mother and father were Shepherds. Charlotte was once a Shepherd, although she stopped many years ago."

"Mrs. Gardner? Vidia's mom?" Zach questioned.

"Yes." Mrs. Santiago paused once more as she was overcome with emotion. "Alas, there is a great deal of danger in this life for us Shepherds. I've lost so much family. My only daughter and her dear husband. My own husband, Hector," Mrs. Santiago drew a deep breath and looked longingly at her granddaughter. "I could go on and on. Sometimes, though, it takes those we care about in other ways. My brother..." Mrs. Santiago clenched her jaw. "He has long been lost to the darkness of it."

"That's how Mom and Dad died? What happened to them?" Aurelia asked, desperately wanting an answer.

"That story is not for today. I will tell you in time." She took Aurelia's hand and looked at her earnestly. "I promise."

Aurelia nodded her head and smiled as she began silently crying. She had waited nearly her entire life to find out what happened to her parents, and the reassurance that she would eventually know was the greatest relief she had ever felt.

Seeing the weight of this news on her granddaughter's face, tears formed at the corners of the gruff old lady's eyes as well. "I'm very sorry you've had to live all these years without your parents. After we lost them, Charlotte and I agreed not to bring you or Vidia into this life. Charlotte left entirely. I still see how heavily your parents' deaths weigh on her. The creatures of the In Between see it too, I'm sure of it. Especially the vultures."

"What do vultures have to do with anything?" Aurelia asked.

"The vultures are the most vile, evil, and powerful creatures from the In Between. Every other creature waits within the shadows of the In Between for its meal, biding its time until those from our world drift in. The vultures, though, can fly between worlds. There are seven of them in total. They are the most haunting of all creatures. Vultures are always on the prowl, hunting within our world and their shadow world. Their appetite is never satiated. These depraved creatures are as old as time, which might explain how they've figured out a way to travel back and forth between their domain and our earthly world."

Mrs. Santiago cringed visibly and continued to speak. "In order for the vulture to stay within our world, they must find a carrier and then a keeper. Their carrier must be an earthly creature, but it cannot be a human. Their keeper, on the other hand, must be human. Once they've found a carrier they can stay, but in order to have any real power they must also connect with their keeper. After they've found their earthly keeper, they become stronger and stronger. And rather than feeding on the wretched souls amongst us who have fallen into the In Between, the vulture can feed on anyone they so please once connected to their keeper."

Mrs. Santiago looked around the room worriedly, then drew a deep breath before she continued. "The longer they stay, the more powerful they become, for a time anyway. They feed on the deadliest of human sins. They wreak havoc on our relationships with our loved ones until we are utterly alone. Eventually the keeper's soul will have completely decayed from within, until they are in such a state of despair that they can no longer function physically. What good is a keeper who is nearly dead and gone forever? So, at this point, the vulture will then bring its haunted keeper back with them to the In Between, trapping them forever and adding to their collection of lost souls. Then the vultures move on to their next keeper, growing their collection and so too their power. I believe that their end goal is to break down the barriers between our two worlds entirely. The vultures are very good at what they do. They have a keen sense of smell and can sense our decaying moralities, but they can only truly feed when we let them in. They push and tempt us, feeding our darkest desires. Once they have been let in, they seep into every corner of our being and rot us to the core."

Mrs. Santiago shook her head. "Dreadful, just dreadful." She paused and thought for a moment. "But even then, I believe there is still hope, however small it may be. Hope is a powerful weapon, and so too is love. And we can never forget that God granted us all free will, did he not? One must never lose hope."

Aurelia's mouth went dry as she remembered the vulture staring at her in the hospital. "We've seen one! A vulture, I mean. It must have made Vidia do all those horrible things! She really hasn't been herself lately." She gulped and held her mother's cross tightly in her hand.

"Did you?" Mrs. Santiago looked at both children suspiciously. "There are many vultures from our world, too. Usually a vulture is just that—a vulture.

These vultures of the In Between are very different. They are strange-looking, large creatures, and they have nearly a human-like appearance to them. Quite grotesque. Their eyes burn you to the core when they stare, and they always bring with them the icy coldness of the In Between."

"I'm sure it was one," Aurelia said, finally feeling as if the bizarre happenings of the last couple of weeks were beginning to make sense.

"Vidia's never been particularly... nice, has she?" Zach questioned hesitantly, and glanced over at Aurelia. "Yeah, but lately she's been especially mean. We've also felt the icy coldness that you just described, a couple times now."

"Yes. It sounds like you have encountered a vulture, young ones. Tell me, was there anything else the Shadow Box spelled, other than Sum Pride and Vultures?"

"Not really. It seemed like it was playing with us though," Aurelia responded.

"Sí. Anything else?"

"That's all we got from the Shadow Box. But when Vidia broke it, she screamed. I think something about pride and leaving us all alone?"

"Leave us be Pride, the child is mine," Zach said uncomfortably, and took another sip of lemonade as Mrs. Santiago once more stared at him.

"Pride? Could he really be back?" Mrs. Santiago mumbled to herself and sighed deeply. "Anything else?" she continued.

"Well, toda—" Zach started as Aurelia quickly cut him off.

"No, that's it."

The old woman pursed her lips and got up to light a prayer candle. "You see now, mija, why St. Jude is so very important to me, and our family. He is the patron saint of the lost." She bowed her head and began the prayer of St. Jude.

"Amen," Aurelia repeated after her grandmother once Mrs. Santiago had finished the prayer. Zach sat quietly and watched the candle flicker wildly in the stillness of the room.

After several minutes of solemn silence, Aurelia quietly spoke up. "Abuela?"

Mrs. Santiago looked up and gave her granddaughter a sad half-smile as she spoke again. "I see all that has happened now. I should have seen it sooner. It all makes sense—Vidia's snake bite, the festering infection, Vidia talking to herself. Her extreme contempt and jealousy over her baby sister. I believe Vidia's snake bite was no coincidence. That snake is a carrier. I have seen snakes used as carriers before."

Zach interrupted Mrs. Santiago. "It's Pride, isn't it? Pride is trying to haunt Vidia, right?"

Mrs. Santiago eyed the boy. "I understand why you might think that, but no, I don't believe so. You said something told Pride to leave Vidia alone. I believe that something was Envy. Envy is attempting to make Vidia its keeper. I fear we are all in great danger, for when one deadly sin is upon us, the others are never far behind. And from the sounds of it we are already dealing with two. I now realize I shielded you for far too long. If I hadn't kept so many secrets, maybe we could have prevented all of this."

Aurelia looked at her grandmother. "I'm sorry, too. We should have told you about what happened with the Shadow Box sooner."

Mrs. Santiago shook her head. "You are telling me now; all we can do is move forward together stronger. No longer will I keep our past from you. I will teach you the ways of a Shepherd, if you so choose to follow in the footsteps of your mother and father and all the Santiagos who have come before you."

"Yes, Abuela, definitely. I've always felt that there was something more to our family, something just beyond my view. It was like I had a calling but didn't know what it was. Now it's starting to make sense." Aurelia's heart raced with excitement and fear as she responded, "I'm ready."

Mrs. Santiago nodded her head. "Sí, sí. I will call your uncle Elvis home from Brazil to help. He's been on a mission there for years, but family comes first. It's time for him to come home. There is much to do. Together, the Santiagos will shepherd as a family once more. We must prepare you." Mrs. Santiago pulled Aurelia in and hugged her.

Aurelia hugged her abuela back tightly as she processed everything.

"I know I'm not a Santiago, but I'm ready to help, too." Zach stood up from the table, standing as tall as he could. "That is, if you'll have me?"

Mrs. Santiago once again stared intensely at Zach. "Yes, young one. I do believe you will be true. You just might make an impressive Shepherd yourself. We're going to need all the help we can get."

"Speaking of help, can we go help Vidia now?" Aurelia questioned, still hugging her abuela.

"We will. For now, though, the most important thing to do is make sure her parents keep her away from Della. I do not believe she has truly become a keeper yet since Frank prevented her from sealing the bond when he stopped Vidia from eating Della, who is clearly Vidia's greatest envy. I'm sure the vulture is not yet finished, though. The Gardners will need to keep Vidia and Della apart, surround Vidia with love, and hope that she finds her way back. If she makes it home safely, we'll bring her into the flock, just as her mother was before her."

Mrs. Santiago stood in thought for a couple of moments. "That is, if Charlotte will allow it." Mrs. Santiago grabbed her purse off the table and put her coat on. "I must share all of this with Charlotte immediately. Now go be children and play."

Her voice then became very stern. "And do not share what we have spoken about with others. The risk is too great."

CHAPTER 16:

PAINS OF OUR PAST

After knocking several times without response, Mrs. Santiago turned the door handle and let herself into the Gardners' house. "Hello? Charlotte? I know you're home. Where are you? We need to talk!" Mrs. Santiago heard a faint voice coming from upstairs.

"I'm up here, in Vidia's room."

Mrs. Santiago climbed the stairs slowly, leaning heavily on the railing. She walked into Vidia's room to find Charlotte sitting on the bed with the lights off, staring blankly into the distance.

"I wondered when you'd be stopping by," Charlotte said in a monotone voice as she continued to stare. "I'm sure you already know what happened. Frank told me you called him in the middle of the night. He doesn't understand how you could have known, but you always do."

Mrs. Santiago took a seat on the bed next to her. "Yes, I hadn't had a feeling of foreboding like that in many years. I had to call. Your family needed me."

"I suppose I should thank you for saving Della. On the other hand, maybe I should blame you for bringing me into this mess all those years ago."

Mrs. Santiago shrugged, shook her head, and sat in silence for a moment before she spoke again. "So, you still haven't told Frank of your past?" Mrs. Santiago asked bluntly.

"Not all of it. Why would I? It's over now. He shouldn't have to carry that burden as well."

"That's why I'm here, Charlotte. I'm afraid it's not over. The vultures have returned once more. This time, though, rather than prey on Annabelle, Victor, Elvis, or you and me, they are coming after the children. Aurelia and that boy Zach just informed me that they used your Shadow Box."

Mrs. Santiago cocked her head to the side and raised her eyebrows. "You know, the one you swore to me that you'd gotten rid of. I told you years ago to destroy that thing, and now your daughter has found it. Vidia, Aurelia, and Zach used it and attempted to contact Annabelle and Victor. The vultures instead answered. Envy and Pride were both there, apparently, and who knows what else. I fear Envy is attempting to haunt your daughter."

"I know," Charlotte responded with despair in her voice. "That's why I've sent Vidia away. She can't be here right now. I can't believe I'm saying this, but I'm not sure she'll ever be able to come back. You should have seen her. My own daughter looked up and smiled at me with her father's finger in her mouth. It's as if she was completely gone. I should have noticed before it was too late, but I failed her. And I'm afraid I'm failing her all over again by sending her away when she clearly needs help."

"Your shepherding instincts are still strong," Mrs. Santiago said nodding her head in approval. "You've done exactly what you must. You need to keep your daughters apart. That's the only way you can protect both of them right now. The only way Envy can make Vidia its keeper is if Vidia harms the source of her innermost jealousy. Right now, that's clearly Della."

"I'll probably have to keep my daughters separated forever." Charlotte hung her head in sorrow. "Vidia is completely gone."

"I believe nobody is ever completely gone, my sweet Charlotte. You must keep hope and love alive. Hope and love are powerful weapons."

"I don't know." Charlotte closed her eyes, searching her mind for a glimmer of hope.

"Hope and love," Mrs. Santiago repeated gently. "After all, it brought you back."

Charlotte sighed. "Sometimes, I'm not so sure. I can still feel it calling me. And what about your brother? We couldn't shepherd him back."

Mrs. Santiago's eyes narrowed with anger. "All the havoc he has willfully caused to our family. So utterly despicable. I suppose you're probably right. Even with hope and love, sometimes the vultures still win." She paused and then continued with a look of worry. "I sense that he has returned home, but that can't be. Elvis spotted him in Brazil, and he is the best tracker we Shepherds have ever seen. He'd certainly know if my brother was back, wouldn't he?"

"Yes. I think so," Charlotte agreed and then went silent for several long seconds. She looked up at Mrs. Santiago briefly before she hung her head in shame and quietly spoke. "We both know your brother wasn't the only one who turned to the darkness." She broke down in tears as she spoke.

Mrs. Santiago pulled Charlotte in and hugged her tightly. "All has been forgiven, Charlotte. There is no need for tears. We need to Shepherd once more. I believe the children are ready."

Charlotte pulled back from Mrs. Santiago's embrace. "No." She shook her head. "No. Never again. I couldn't handle that life when I was younger, and Vidia is so much like I was. I need to protect her. I need to protect my family."

"But Charlotte, what other choice do we have now? The vultures are back."

"No, Esmeralda," Charlotte repeated staunchly. She had never called Mrs. Santiago by her first name before but wanted to show her how very serious she was.

"Alright. I'll respect your wishes, but please, just think about it. The vultures are back. We can't hide from them any longer," Mrs. Santiago said softly. "Remember, Charlotte, a Shepherd's path must be started while still a child, or the ability to consciously travel to the In Between is lost forever. I fear we are going to need another generation of Shepherds very soon, especially if my brother Felix has returned. I'm sure he will want revenge."

"There has to be another way," Charlotte said miserably. "They're just children. We shouldn't put this on them."

"A shepherd fully accepts their burden and never complains." Mrs. Santiago held her head high as she spoke. "It's time to teach the children. We need to get them ready."

"No. It's not fair. They're just children and have no idea what they're being pulled into. You nearly lost everything. Your daughter, son-in-law, brother..." her voice cracked and she trailed off. "And... you know about what happened to me. If I couldn't bear it, what makes you think my eleven-year-old daughter can? This is just the beginning, and I've already had to send her away from home. I can't imagine how lonely and awful she must feel right now."

Mrs. Santiago pulled Charlotte back into her embrace. "Vidia isn't alone. She is with family who love her. And I will watch over her as well. I'll do everything I can to shepherd Vidia back." As Mrs. Santiago held Charlotte, she was overwhelmed with the painful memory of an embrace they shared years ago on the day Annabelle was lost. Tears streamed down Mrs. Santiago's weathered cheeks at the memory of her daughter and son-in-law, and the two women wept together.

CHAPTER 17:

HOMECOMING

"Good morning, Vidia. What brings you in today?" Reverend Francis asked curiously.

Vidia spoke quietly, her voice trembling. "I wanted to talk to you about something... something terrible that I have done."

"We all make mistakes. Tell me more," Reverend Francis said.

"I envied my sister so much, it drove me to a horrible state. I wanted so badly to get rid of her that I... I..." Vidia paused.

"It's all right, Vidia, these conversations are never easy. It can be hard to acknowledge our wrongdoings, but don't worry. This is not a place of judgment, but rather a place of forgiveness."

Vidia continued slowly. "I couldn't... I couldn't

handle sharing Mom and Dad's love. For eleven years it had just been the three of us, and I didn't know what it felt like not to be the center of attention. It made me so angry and jealous. So, I decided I was going to make things go back to the way they were before my sister came along. I decided I was going to get rid of her, and I decided I was going to do that by..." She paused again for a couple of long seconds before continuing. "By eating her."

A look of shock ran across the Reverend's face, but he remained silent as she continued.

"But something else happened. I accidentally bit off my father's finger. I didn't mean to, but that's not an excuse. My jealousy was so out of control that I hurt my dad. I think I may have ruined things for my entire family, but I want to fix everything. I need to. I want to be a good sister and a good daughter." Vidia had been staring down at her lap, and finally looked at the Reverend with desperation in her sad green eyes.

Reverend Francis was horrified by what he had just heard, but he could also see the pain on Vidia's face. He cleared his throat and then calmly responded. "God forgives those who are truly repentant and ask for his forgiveness. Are you repentant?"

"Yes," Vidia responded, and then turned her gaze away from the Reverend, too ashamed to look him in the eye any longer.

"Then God has forgiven you," the Reverend said with a head nod.

"But what about my mom and dad?" Vidia questioned.

He thought for a moment and said, "In my experience, parents always forgive their children. But sometimes that can take a little time."

The reverend recited a couple of prayers and instructed Vidia to say a few of her own. He then sent her on her way.

"How did it go?" Dad asked Vidia somberly as she exited the church doors.

"It was good. I'm glad I did it," Vidia said, feeling as if a weight had been lifted off her shoulders.

"I'm surprised you wanted to talk to him. That took a lot of courage," Dad said, looking at Vidia curiously.

"I'm taking responsibility for what I did. I'm done hiding from it," Vidia said as she climbed into the car.

"I'm proud of you, honey, but I know that wasn't really you that night. You weren't in your right mind. The venom caused you to hallucinate. I should have noticed the snake bite getting worse. If only I'd taken you to the doctor when you were first bitten, I know you wouldn't have done any of that." Dad sighed as he started the car.

"Maybe you're right, Dad. That infection got pretty nasty." As the words came out of Vidia's mouth, she was unsure of herself and wondered how different her life might be if she hadn't been bitten by the snake. *Maybe I wouldn't have done anything differently,* she thought, full of worry.

Dad glanced in the rear-view mirror and caught Vidia's eyes in his as she stared. "So, you ready to finally go home? Mom and Della are waiting for you. We've told Della all about her big sister. She even says your name now. She can't wait to see you again."

Vidia nodded enthusiastically, too overwhelmed to verbalize a response. It had been more than a year since that tragic Halloween. That night still haunted Vidia's dreams constantly. Some of the events were hazy in her memory, but other parts she remembered very clearly. She remembered sitting in her sister's crib. She also recalled wanting to eat her sister, but couldn't entirely remember why. She couldn't remember biting her father, but she could still practically taste his bloody finger in her mouth. She had a visceral reaction to this memory and gagged every time she thought about it, wanting nothing more than to erase it from her mind forever. She vividly remembered the horror in her father's eyes when he saw her infected ankle and rushed her to the hospital. She couldn't understand how her father's only concern in that moment was for her and not his own severed finger. Her mother's panicked screams still echoed through her mind.

Vidia sat in the car, attempting to push these thoughts away as best she could. She instead diverted her attention to all that had happened since that Halloween. She spent over a week at the hospital being treated with antibiotics. Dad was there the whole time, feeling terribly guilty and apologizing for not noticing the infection sooner. Mom came and went from the hospital, but even when she was there, she treated Vidia much differently than Dad. She seemed withdrawn and depressed.

On the last night at the hospital, Vidia overheard Mom talking to Dad while she pretended to be sleeping. "There's no way we can bring her home to Della. Frank, there's no excuse for what she did. Stop trying to blame it all on the snake bite."

"Not in front of Vidia. What if she wakes up?" Dad responded.

The next day, Vidia was released from the hospital, and her parents shared the most heartbreaking news she could have imagined. She was going to stay with her grandparents at their house for a while. As Mom said goodbye to Vidia and handed her a suitcase of clothes, she pulled her in close and whispered into her ear, "'Peccatum, be gone.' I want you to say that whenever you don't feel like yourself." Vidia didn't understand but nodded in agreement, hoping to gain her mother's approval.

Dad decided to stay with Vidia nearly every weekend, despite the three-hour drive to and from his parents' home. On Monday mornings, he'd wake up before the sun and make the long drive home to be with Mom and Della for the week while he worked. Mom only visited her briefly a few times within the past year and never with Della. Things with her mom just weren't the same anymore. Vidia hoped and prayed that her relationship with her mother could be healed, but as the weeks and months wore on, she felt more and more discouraged.

Grandma and Grandpa had been very loving and warm with Vidia while she lived with them. Vidia had even grown to love their calico cat, Lulu. Vidia never had much of an opinion on the cat in the past, and Lulu seemed rather uninterested in Vidia as well. When Vidia first arrived at her grandparents' home after leaving the hospital, Lulu's hair stood on end at the sight of her, and she hissed. *She knows I'm crazy,* Vidia thought dejectedly. But within a few months, Lulu had become Vidia's constant companion, following her around everywhere. Her grandparents never let Lulu into their bedroom, but Vidia welcomed her happily.

Nighttime was much less lonely away from home when she had Lulu by her side, snuggled up and purring softly. Vidia was comforted by the many similarities between her grandparents and her father. So many of her grandpa's mannerisms were nearly identical to her father's. Although Vidia longed for her mom and dad, she eventually felt that her grandparents' home was her home away from home.

Life moved at a much slower pace than in Foggy Hollows. The past year had involved a lot of reading and time outside. The library was only a short walk from her grandparents' house, and it became Vidia's new favorite place. The only time TV was allowed was for the evening news or when Grandpa was watching one of his sports games. Vidia had protested, but eventually grew to appreciate it, taking a newfound interest in current events and baseball.

Grandpa took to playing poker with Vidia, and Grandma had even taught her how to knit, something she was surprised to find helped calm her nerves. Every few days, she walked with her grandmother to a tiny garden market to pick up their groceries and occasionally buy plants for their garden. Life felt simpler here, easier, more soothing. Still, it was very hard not living with her parents full-time. Vidia even desperately ached to see her baby sister again and looked back on her past behavior with intense revulsion, as if it couldn't have really been her that was so filled with animosity. It had been a strange, difficult year, and she longed to be back home with her family and friends. She realized in hindsight the comfort she had felt in her home, especially in her yard, and pined for her swing under the live oak tree. Her spot.

She wondered what Aurelia and Zach were up to, and if they'd found new friends since she left. She was convinced that when she returned home, she'd find out that she had been forgotten, an outcast even among the outcasts.

Once Halloween rolled around the following year, and Vidia still wasn't home, she didn't celebrate at all, except to hand out candy for her grandparents. Halloween carried a bleak heaviness for her now when it was once her favorite holiday. Dad drove up and offered to take Vidia trick-or-treating, but she politely declined, claiming she was now too old. She knew in her heart that if it wasn't for what had happened last Halloween, she'd want to trick or treat until she was no longer allowed. Now it just felt wrong, especially without Aurelia. They had gone trick-or-treating together every year for as long as she could remember.

Sometimes late at night on the weekends, she'd sneak out of her bedroom, sit against the old metal railing, and count the peculiar flowers that adorned the wallpaper in her grandparents' hallway. She spent many of these nights staring intently at the old pictures of Dad from his childhood that littered the staircase walls. Mostly, though, she'd eavesdrop on Dad's conversations with Grandma and Grandpa into the late hours of the night. She loved listening in on the grown-up talk, which usually centered around her family that she missed back at home.

Some nights she'd hear her father on the phone with Mom. This is when she paid the most attention. Usually, the main topic at hand was whatever Della had done that day. Vidia listened attentively, trying her hardest to understand the conversation based on what she could hear. She deeply regretted her actions and longed for another shot at being a big sister. These phone conversations helped her feel a little closer to her sister.

Every so often, she heard her parents arguing. "Of course I want to be home, but I need to be here, too," Dad would say. Or, "I'm sorry you're dealing with Della on your own again this weekend." Then Dad would usually follow up with, "Why haven't you come to visit Vidia lately?" which only seemed to escalate the disagreement. These arguments were always very difficult for Vidia to hear and made her realize how hard the year must have been on her parents, too.

After she had listened in on these disagreements, she'd retreat to her bedroom, sit on her bed, pull her baby blanket over her head, and wait for the sinking feeling in the pit of her stomach to subside. It was nearly impossible for her to bear the weight of feeling that she was the cause of her parents' arguments. Her scar from her snake bite was completely healed, but in these anxious moments, it itched intensely, and she couldn't stop herself from scratching as she drifted off to sleep.

On these restless nights when she finally fell asleep, her dreams felt so vivid it was as if she wasn't asleep at all. These night terrors always had the same theme, but the duration and details varied slightly each time. She'd find herself lying in bed in what she thought was her grandparents' house, but something about it filled her with an overwhelming sense of dread.

She'd sit up in her bed, feeling colder than she had ever experienced in her waking life. The icy air stung and bit at her face as if she was in the arctic. Sitting in the corner of her room, she'd see

Mrs. Santiago's calavera that had so captivated her last Halloween. It looked and smelled fresh as could be, as if it had been carved only minutes ago. Although it was not lit, Vidia felt an ever-so-slight warmth when she placed her hand on the pumpkin.

She'd hold her baby blanket tightly and tiptoe out of her room to explore the old house. The house was no longer cluttered with Grandma's homey, mismatched style. The warm, welcoming feeling was completely obliterated and replaced with a barren and empty void. It was almost as if the house itself was being suffocated, silently crying out in despair. The pictures on the walls were all gone, and the flowers that adorned the hallway wallpaper were shriveled and dead. The familiar smells she had become accustomed to were missing, and her grandparents could no longer be found.

No matter how many pieces of clothing she put on during these dreams, she just couldn't escape the cold. At this point, Vidia would become panicked and try to escape, only to find every door and window locked. She'd look out the window to see a constant drizzle of rain through a foggy haze and a blanket of ice covering the ground. No matter what, V always eventually appeared and beckoned Vidia to take her bony, clawed hand. These were the only moments Vidia saw or heard V since that fateful Halloween night. She seemed bigger now, and moved with more force and strength. Vidia would try to cry out for help, but no noise would come. She'd run through the house to hide, but V would follow and find her.

Eventually, Vidia would retreat into her room, lock her door, and begin to pray in desperation as she heard V's footsteps getting closer and closer. For reasons Vidia could not explain, the calavera lit itself every time she began praying. A warmth filled the room as the calavera burned brighter and brighter and Vidia's prayers became louder and louder. The pumpkin then engulfed itself in flames, and V shrieked from outside the room as if she was the Wicked Witch of the West and melting away. Vidia watched as the pumpkin burnt into ashes, and suddenly a blazing torch appeared in its place. Vidia stepped closer for a better look, and she noticed a small hand gripping the torch. The torch burned brighter and brighter as it rotated in a circular motion, and a peculiar popping sound echoed through the room. Vidia recognized the bizarre noise, recollecting her wild encounter with the crazy old man on Halloween morning. The torch then stopped spinning, and the hand let go of it.

Strangely, rather than fall to the ground, the torch remained suspended in the air as if propped up by something invisible, which made no sense to Vidia even in her dreams. The one hand was then joined by another, protruding through the air above the pumpkin's ashes. The hands calmly gripped either side of the emptiness around them and pulled, and a sound similar to fabric tearing reverberated throughout the room. Mrs. Santiago then carefully climbed through the incision she made and into the room. As she emerged, the opening behind her closed and the corner of Vidia's room reappeared as if nothing had happened. Mrs. Santiago then plucked the suspended torch from the air, took Vidia's hand in hers, and whispered calmly, "You're not alone, Vidia."

At this point, V would rip Vidia's bedroom door off its hinges. Once she saw Mrs. Santiago, she would scream in anger, spew venomously in unfamiliar tongues, and try with all her might to charge into the bedroom. Each time V lunged towards them, Mrs. Santiago waved the flaming torch from side to side, as if putting an invisible barricade in place while holding tightly onto Vidia's hand. The creature remained at the door's threshold, hissing, growling, and thrashing maniacally.

"Darling," Mrs. Santiago would again whisper into Vidia's ear, "It's time for us to go home. Repeat after me. Peccatum, be gone." Vidia would do as instructed, feeling comforted as she recalled her mother using these same words. In these moments, Vidia felt completely protected by Mrs. Santiago, despite V's terrifying hysterics. Once she felt content and safe, she'd wake from her dream. Or so she'd think. After these nightmares, she awoke groggily to Mrs. Santiago sitting by her bedside holding her hand. "Sleep, child. The In Between is behind us for the night," Mrs. Santiago would whisper kindly.

The first time Vidia had this nightmare, Mrs. Santiago quietly called for Lulu, clicking her tongue several times. "Here, Lulu, come Miss Lulu." Within a couple of seconds, Lulu jumped up onto Vidia's bed. "Now, Lulu, I want you to stay with Vidia. Can you do that for me?"

Lulu stared at Vidia cautiously and looked at Mrs. Santiago as if for approval.

"Yes, kitty," Mrs. Santiago said encouragingly. Lulu then meowed sweetly and curled up against Vidia's chest, purring softly as she settled. "You are never alone, Vidia. Love will keep you safe. Now sleep peacefully."

Then the old woman would rise to her feet and quietly walk out of her bedroom. Vidia vividly remembered the first time this happened and how surprised she was that the cat had laid on her. Lulu's soft fuzzy body warmed hers and its purring soothed Vidia's troubled nerves in a way she had not expected. After each of these incidents, Vidia eventually fell back asleep until morning.

Once dawn broke, she would rise and head downstairs, expecting to see Mrs. Santiago had come to visit, but she'd instead be greeted by her grandparents at the breakfast table. Vidia concluded, somewhat confusedly, that the bizarre events of these nights were simply bad dreams, and Mrs. Santiago at her bedside must have been a dream within a dream. She was surprised that of all the people in the world, Mrs. Santiago was the one who rescued her in these nightmares, but she appreciated it all the same. She felt as though the old woman's presence somehow prevented her terrible dreams from becoming reality.

As Vidia sat in the backseat of the old Jeep with her dad, she propped her feet up and sighed with relief. She hadn't experienced one of these awful dreams in several months and hoped they would never return. That morning, before she left for home, Vidia found Lulu waiting for her by the front door. Vidia bent down and hugged the cat goodbye and kissed her forehead.

"I'm going to miss you, Lulu," she said. "Thanks for everything."

Lulu flopped onto her back, showing her large pregnant belly to Vidia, who laughed at the sight.

"I wish I wasn't going to miss these cute little kitties coming. You'll love being a mommy. I'm headed home to be with mine."

The three-hour drive home felt especially slow as they plunked down the old country roads. The seconds ticked into minutes, and the minutes into hours. Dad asked her several times if she wanted to hear any music or talk, but Vidia said no. She felt the silence almost obligatory for such a momentous occasion.

As they finally turned down the street that led to their house, Dad reached back and took Vidia's hand in his. "I love you, Vidia, always. Mom does, too. And guess what, your little sister Della can't wait to see you."

Vidia looked down at her dad's hand on hers. She observed the jagged, ugly scar running around his index finger and her stomach turned with disgust. Then she wondered how anyone's love could be so unconditional. She squeezed his hand and replied quietly. "I love you too, Dad."

As their house came into view, Vidia saw Mom standing in the yard, waiting and waving from underneath the old live oak tree that stood steadfast, just as grand as she remembered, waiting for Vidia to come home. On the swing next to Mom, she saw Della, but her little sister wasn't alone. Aurelia swung back and forth gently holding Della. She gazed down at the baby lovingly, then looked up and waved excitedly to Vidia. The all too familiar creeping, hateful feeling of envy started to take hold in Vidia's gut and seeped into her mind.

What is she doing here? And why is she holding my sister and sitting on my swing? Vidia's snake bite started to pulsate painfully, and Vidia squeezed down hard on her father's hand. *No. I need to be rational. There's no reason for me to be angry.*

If Vidia had looked very carefully at the large tree branch above the swing, she would have noticed the same muddy brown snake that had bitten her last year. It sat languidly, curled up on a branch hidden from plain sight, sunbathing in the cool morning air. Above its curled-up body, the creature's head was fully visible, and a diamond-shaped crimson spot adorned the center of its forehead. The snake repeatedly flicked its tongue, analyzing the smells in the air, patiently waiting for the scent of the very specific prey it was hunting. It sat, undetected, watching the heartfelt reunion scrupulously with excited malice in its eyes.

I'm finally back. My whole family is waiting for me, Vidia thought. *And my best friend even came over, too.*

After over a year of never quite feeling at home, a calmness and sense of belonging warmed Vidia to the core. As this sense of repose washed over her, the harshness of her features softened, and she looked toward her family and friend with a kindness in her bright green eyes.

"Finally. We're back," Vidia whispered to herself.

As Dad parked the car and turned off the ignition, Vidia locked eyes with her mom. They stared at each other for a moment. Panic suddenly flooded Vidia, imagining rejection from her own mother. Within another second, this feeling passed as a warm smile lit up Mom's face.

Everything is ok, Vidia thought. She threw open the car door and jumped into her mom's waiting arms, embracing her mother with all of her might, never wanting to let go. Neither said a word for several moments.

Mom finally broke the silence. "I was so worried we might have lost you. I'm glad you're home now. We've missed you so much."

Vidia knew her mother was not one to wear her emotions on her sleeve, so these words meant everything to her. "I've missed you so much too, Mom," Vidia replied as she continued to hug her tightly. *Maybe things can go back to normal now,* she thought.

Vidia felt a tug at her leg. She turned to see Della, staring up at her. She smiled at her little sister, bent down and picked her up lovingly. Della pushed her face against Vidia's, smiling broadly and pulling at her big sister's cheeks. Then she hooked one of her chubby little fingers into her sister's mouth and laughed playfully. Vidia gently pulled it out and laughed along with her, happy to be holding her little sister and looking forward to getting to know her.

Aurelia smiled, pushing her big glasses back into position on her face as she swung back and forth. "I was worried I wouldn't recognize you anymore, but you look the same! Well, a little taller."

Vidia's expression suddenly became very serious. "Who said you could use my swing while I was gone?" she questioned, putting her free hand on her hip. Before Aurelia could respond, Vidia laughed at herself. "Just kidding, I missed you!"

As Vidia held Della, Mom put her arms around her two daughters, and Dad embraced Mom.

"Well, this looks like a picture-perfect family reunion," Aurelia said, watching the family hug.

"Get in here, you." Mrs. Gardner smiled at Aurelia, motioning toward her.

Aurelia jumped off the swing and joined the hug. Everyone stood together in the cool breeze of the new day. A sensation Vidia had never before experienced swept over her all at once. An immense feeling of gratitude filled her heart as she stood there in the warm embrace of family.

"This is right where I belong. I'm home," Vidia sighed softly.

CHAPTER 18:

Vidia's Revelation

The excitement of Vidia's homecoming began to settle as the day drew near its end and dusk crept onto the horizon. Vidia ate a delicious dinner, courtesy of Dad, and unpacked all her things from Grandma and Grandpa's house. Now that she was settled, she knew exactly what she wanted to do. She slipped out the front door and walked over to the large live oak tree.

"I've really missed you," she said, putting a hand on its massive trunk. Then she sat down on her swing. "And I've missed you even more." She gripped the ropes forcefully as she pushed off the ground and began to sway back and forth.

Almost as quickly as she started swinging, something touched her back shoulder. Vidia screamed in horror as her mind flashed back to the snake bite. She jumped off the swing, stumbling, and twirled around to defend herself.

"Zach! Ugh, why do you always do that? I was about to punch you in the face just now."

"I've heard that before," Zack laughed, shaking his head.

"What are you doing here?" Vidia questioned, now slightly embarrassed and very irritated.

"I invited him," Aurelia said, popping out from behind the tree. "We've been waiting and waiting to find some time alone with you since you got back. We have to tell you something!"

"You sure are jumpy. I didn't mean to scare you," Zach said, raising his eyebrows up and down goofily, clearly still messing with Vidia.

"I wasn't scared at all. Just wanted to make sure it wasn't another snake."

"Oh, right, yeah, that would be really bad," Zach agreed.

"Vidia, you're not listening!" Aurelia was breathless with excitement as she spoke. "We've got news. Huge news! Wait until you hear all this. You're never going to believe it! Or, I guess maybe you will because it makes sense of all the crazy things that happened last year. I've been waiting a year—actually, more than a year now—to tell you!" Aurelia persisted.

"Come back tomorrow morning and tell me. And not with him," Vidia said, glaring at Zach.

"Aw, man. You didn't miss me even a little?" Zach questioned, smiling. "We missed you. Things aren't as fun around here without your constant complaining." He smirked at his joke.

A small grin crept across Vidia's face. "Well, I guess I missed you a little, too," she admitted.

"You guys aren't listening to me! Come on now!" Aurelia threw her hands in the air in frustration.

Realizing they had veered off topic, Zach turned toward Aurelia. "Sorry, Ellie. She's right, Vidia. You gotta hear this." His face suddenly grew somber, and he gulped before he spoke again. "It's really important you never tell anyone else about it though. Ever. We've been sworn to secrecy."

"When did you start calling her Ellie?" Vidia wrinkled her nose. Before Zach could answer, Vidia turned to Aurelia. "And when did you start sharing secrets with Zach over me?" she said, feeling both jealous and hurt.

"Vidia, I've wanted to tell you so badly! But you were gone," Aurelia explained apologetically. "I wanted you to know more than anyone."

"Enough with the chit chat. Let's get on with it already. We need to get you up to speed!" Zach put his hand on his head, now as exasperated as Aurelia.

"Ok. Just go on and tell me. This better be good," Vidia said, her hands crossed and eyes narrowed.

Aurelia looked around to make sure they were alone and motioned for Vidia to come closer. Vidia instinctively reciprocated and the three children gathered close under the canopy of the tree. Aurelia shared everything she knew about the In Between, all that resided there, the Santiagos' history of shepherding, and Vidia's mother's involvement when she was younger. Vidia sat silently, taking it all in. Once she was done, Aurelia hugged Vidia and apologized.

"I'm so sorry I didn't know this sooner. If you hadn't come over to help me find out more about my parents, if you hadn't played with the Shadow Box... Maybe you wouldn't of, wouldn't of... well, you know."

"Wouldn't of what?" Vidia questioned, not following.

"She's trying to say maybe you wouldn't have temporarily gone crazy and tried to eat your sister," Zach said, looking sideways at Vidia.

Vidia glared at Zach for a moment and then turned to Aurelia again as if she hadn't heard him. "This wasn't your fault, Aurelia. You know that right?" Vidia spoke softly, surprising even herself with her heartfelt words. "I'm responsible for my actions."

"I've been trying to tell her it's not her fault," Zach agreed.

"Well, I should have realized you needed help. I knew something was off," Aurelia countered.

"What? You couldn't have known about any of this," Vidia concluded. "So..." Vidia paused, trying to collect her thoughts and understand the full scope of the situation at hand. "Your grandma believes that the deadly sin of envy has chosen me to be its, what's the word you used, keeper? Does that mean the voice inside my head is Envy? How can it be both a vulture and inside my head?"

"The voice is Envy. I think Envy chose the snake to be its carrier, and then you to be its keeper. The snake bite is what let Envy in. It's there, inside you, talking to you, pushing for you to let it take control. It probably took control the night you tried to hurt Della, or at least partially. My abuela thinks it's still in you, but that you have gotten it under control, for now anyways. We're not entirely sure how it all works, but my abuela is sure that if we can find the carrier, we'll be one step closer to figuring this all out."

"We've been looking and looking everywhere for that sucker," Zach chimed in, shaking his head. "No dice yet, but we'll find that snake, I'm sure of it."

"How do you know who the carrier is anyway?" Vidia inquired.

"It's not easy," Zach continued, "but there's always a red marking on a carrier's forehead. Mrs. Santiago also told us your dad said it was a huge snake. So that makes it easier. How many huge snakes can there be around here? Carriers are always abnormally large for their species."

A couple of moments of silence followed before Vidia spoke again. "So, you basically think I'm being controlled by a bird?" she asked, sounding offended.

"No. It's not that simple. The word my abuela used was haunted, but your dad stopped it when he pulled you out of the crib, I think?" Aurelia said, sounding a little confused.

"I'm not haunted! I am completely in control now. I haven't even heard V for months!"

"Why do you sound so angry? I mean, isn't this a better explanation than you just being crazy?" Zach questioned.

"I don't understand why you're even here and privy to all this information, Zach," Vidia said, still miffed at the suggestion that something else could possibly be controlling her. "It's like the two of you have some sort of secret club."

"The three of us are in this together, Vidia. We'd never do this without you," Aurelia assured her.

"It is a secret, you're right about that," Zach said. "I know we already said this, but it's important to repeat. We can't tell anyone who is not already a part of it. That includes your mom, Vidia, but only because she said no to you shepherding. We need to wait until she agrees to it. We're working on her."

"Wait, what did my mom say?" Vidia's eyes narrowed.

"My abuela told us that your mom does not want to bring you into this life. She says it's too dangerous and won't put that burden on you." Aurelia sounded disappointed as she quietly responded.

"I'll decide what's too dangerous for me," Vidia snapped. "My mom and all her secrets. Maybe I don't want to be part of a secret club where everyone thinks I'm being controlled by a vulture." She paused, stamping her foot in protest as she thought. "Or... maybe I do, just to prove everyone wrong. But I'll make that decision for myself. It's not my mom's to make."

"Not controlled, haunted," Zach interrupted. "By the vulture Envy."

Vidia rolled her eyes at Zach. "Haunted. Controlled. What's the difference?"

"My understanding is that you are still yourself, but the vulture is very powerful and constantly trying to corrupt you, if that makes sense. Normalizing the bad, influencing you to do... its bidding, I guess. The vulture searches for a keeper who has tendencies similar to their own, and pokes and prods at you, trying to make you crazy. Eventually, if the vulture wins, you become completely haunted. Once the keeper is haunted, the vulture's power really takes hold and begins to grow. It feeds off its keeper's soul and takes whatever it wants, destroying everything in its path."

Zach thought for a moment and then continued. "It's not natural, though. A human can only contain that much evil for so long before their earthly body collapses and they die. The vultures won't let that happen though, since they'd then lose the soul they worked so hard for. So right before death takes hold, the vulture returns to the In Between with its keeper, trapping them in a state that's neither alive nor dead, forever. Each of the seven vultures has their own collection of lost souls, and each soul they take increases their power and size. Even after they've finished with you, used you to the point of no return, they still won't release you. They just add you to their collection of used-up souls. Then the vulture moves on and looks for its next victim. But sometimes the vultures are not successful in their attempts at haunting us. If their prey proves to be stronger than they anticipated, the vulture eventually gives up and moves on to someone new. Even then, though, there is still a connection between the vulture and its potential keeper. That connection will remain intact for as long as the carrier still roams. Mrs. Santiago thinks this is what has happened to you since V is gone. At least for now," Zach finished, pleased with his explanation.

"So... I am in control?" Vidia questioned.

Aurelia nodded her head, "Well yeah, but not like normal." She gestured expressively as she tried to put her thoughts into words. After a moment she spoke. "It's like you're standing knee deep in the ocean and the undercurrent is trying to drag you out to sea. The moment you stop trying your hardest to fight it, the sea will take you. Does that make sense?" Aurelia questioned.

Vidia's eyes filled with tears. "It does. More than you can ever imagine. Everything makes so much more sense now. I thought I was going crazy and was afraid to tell anyone." She paused and looked at both her friends, still choked up. "It feels good to say that out loud."

"Don't cry, Vidia. We're going to help you and you're going to be okay." Aurelia stretched her arms out with tears in her eyes and Vidia went in to hug her friend.

After a moment, Vidia withdrew and crossed her arms. "It's still annoying that Zach knew about all this before me. You should have told me sooner. Do you know how horrible this has been?"

"Of course you were the first person I wanted to tell. But you weren't here. We did sneak in to see you at the hospital. But that was before we knew," Aurelia said, hoping her friend would finally understand.

"Yeah," Zach added. "We found out that night, and we tried to come back the next day, but you were gone. You'd been discharged, and your dad took you to your grandparents."

"I was only three hours away," Vidia protested. "You could have found a way to visit me at least once to tell me. Write me a letter. Do anything. I was gone a whole year."

"Abuela said we were not allowed to contact you at all," Aurelia responded. "She was very serious about it. She said it was a matter of life and death for both you and us. Apparently, if Envy knew you understood what it was doing, it could have become even more destructive and you were still on the brink of losing yourself. Abuela promised us that she'd do everything possible to shepherd you back. She's the reason you're allowed to come home. She told your mom it was time to bring you back to Foggy Hollows. I'm not sure if you knew when you were in the In Between since a lot of people don't, but Abuela says it's been months since she's found you there."

Vidia thought for a couple of moments, recalling how Mrs. Santiago appeared in what she thought were just strangely vivid dreams, but now realized she must have been in the In Between. Her strong dislike for the old lady melted away entirely. She sat down on the ground, unable to digest this new information fully without a long moment of silence.

"The In Between sort of felt like a nightmare to me. A cold, realistic nightmare. Your abuela rescued me in all of them. I haven't had one of those for months. I guess the In Between is different for everyone, then?"

"Yes, that's what Abuela says. A lot of people have absolutely no idea when they are there. Some people feel like they're hallucinating. But it's a cold, eerie place. And there are horrible creatures in it. But most people trapped there aren't haunted, or even bad. We still aren't even sure why some people are there. You can ask Abuela about it." Aurelia paused. "Well, if your mom agrees to let you be a Shepherd."

"Ok, ok, enough with the chit chat. Now you know everything we know. Let's get to the big question. Are you in or out?" Zach asked bluntly.

"I'm in," Vidia responded. "And nobody, not even my mom gets to say otherwise."

Aurelia jumped into the air with a huge smile on her face, her fists balled up in excitement. "Yes! I'm so glad! I'm sure we can get Uncle Elvis to convince your mom, even if Abuela can't. He was good friends with her when they were younger."

"Uncle Elvis?" Vidia asked.

"He's another one of the Santiago Shepherds. Huge dude. Not someone you'd want to mess with," Zach explained.

"No," Aurelia said lightheartedly, laughing at Zach's description. "He's just a big teddy bear. And the best uncle. He was working in Brazil for years and just got back," Aurelia commented. "I think you'll really like him. He keeps saying we all need to start before we get too old and it's too late."

"Why too late?" Vidia asked.

"You can only become a Shepherd as a child. I don't really get it. Uncle Elvis and Abuela haven't said why. But that is why it's so important we convince your mom soon," Aurelia responded.

"We've got a lot to learn, and we need you with us," Zach said, nodding his head in agreement with Aurelia.

"Alright, then. It's settled. With or without my mom's approval," Vidia announced. She climbed back on her swing and began swaying. "I need some time by myself to think about all this. Let's meet up tomorrow and figure out our next move."

"That sounds great. See you tomorrow. We're so happy you're back. I can't tell you how relieved I am that you know everything now." Aurelia smiled.

"Glad you're in, Vidia," Zach said enthusiastically. "Three is a powerful number. That's what Mrs. Santiago told us."

With that, Zach and Aurelia climbed onto their bikes and rode off.

The dusky evening sky had given way to darkness, but Vidia continued swinging as she contemplated the events of the evening. Although Aurelia and Zach had long since left, a strong sensation that she was being watched swept over her. She looked around vigilantly, feeling very vulnerable. She was unable to see much of anything with only a few dimly lit lampposts in the distance.

That snake could be anywhere, she thought as she began to panic.

She collected herself and decided that if anyone was actually watching her, the last thing she wanted was to let her fear show.

"I know you're still here, V," Vidia called out loudly. "You're done. Done messing up my life! I won't allow it any longer. Do you hear me? V? Or should I say En-V!? Envy? Answer me!" Vidia bellowed, now finding her courage. "Go ahead and show yourself. I'm not scared of you!"

Nothing but silence followed. Even the crickets ceased their incessant chirps, and Vidia's thoughts remained her own.

"Guess you're scared," Vidia said cooly, and as the taunt came out of her mouth, she realized she shouldn't be so brazen.

Within a couple of moments, she heard the

pitter-patter of light rain as it began to fall around the large tree, and a breeze picked up the chilly drizzle, sprinkling the icy droplets onto her face.

Time to go inside, Vidia thought to herself.

Before she had a chance to jump off the swing and head inside, she heard the sharp cawing of a bird. She looked up and every bone in her body was chilled to the core as an enormous vulture soared down from the sky and landed on the highest branch of the live oak tree. The creature stared down at Vidia, and its beady red eyes glowed unnaturally in the haze of the night. As she looked at the vulture, she realized its face somehow looked eerily similar to hers. Vidia hopped off the swing, heart racing, and picked up a large rock. She looked at the bird, giving it her best menacing glare, and with every ounce of strength she had, hurled the rock at the creature. The rock sailed past the tree, narrowly missing her target. The bird remained still as a statue upon its perch, completely unfazed.

A bright bolt of lightning flashed across the night sky, illuminating the vulture's face. Vidia noticed its expression clearly changing, now looking pleased as it observed her. Envy's evil eyes became brighter as they bored into Vidia's, and its twisted smile beckoned as if it was calling her home.

"I am home, and you can't take me away. You're nothing but a parasite," Vidia yelled, her breath visible in the cold darkness.

Before she could speak again, a roaring crack of thunder shook the ground beneath her, and the sheer force behind it startled her intensely. The hair on the back of her neck stood on end, and she clumsily stumbled towards her house, making sure not to take her eye off the bird for even a second. Her ankle began to itch, and as she resisted the urge to scratch it, she felt a powerful yearning to embrace the foul otherworldly being that continued to glare at her. Sickened with her thoughts, Vidia shuddered and felt a rising wave of nausea.

The bird stared on, clearly pleased with its effect on her. It cawed loudly, summoning her back. Vidia backed up farther toward her house as Envy continued to caw repeatedly and more forcefully with each step Vidia took. After what felt like an eternity, Vidia reached the safety of her front door. She fumbled with the door handle for a couple of moments and stepped inside. Her courage returned as she crossed the threshold and felt relieved in the comfort of her home.

"I know what you want now! I am my own keeper and no one else's. I'm in control!" she screamed out the open door at the creature, stomping her foot.

The bird cocked its pale white head to the side, and its cawing seemed to morph into a bizarre, maniacal laughter. It opened its wings menacingly, revealing itself to be larger than Vidia with ugly, balding black feathers. It leapt off its perch and circled atop Vidia's house several times and then flew off, vanishing into the dreary night.

Vidia could hear its laughter growing fainter in the distance until it was replaced with the unnerving popping sound Vidia was now growing familiar with. The noise echoed into the night and faded away. Vidia stood in her doorway and listened intently, waiting for any further signs of the vulture. She was relieved that all she heard was the pitter-patter of rain.

Vidia retreated inside her house, breathing deeply as she locked the door behind her. "Safe and sound. At least for now," she sighed.